FINAL WARNING

Not more than a few moments passed when the man and Amanda appeared, his horse going full out. Fargo saw the man frown as he cast another glance behind him. Eyes narrowed, Fargo focused on the horse's feet. When the mount's left forefoot went over the rope, he yanked the lariat up, pulled it taut with all his strength.

The man pitched forward as he was tripped and Fargo saw the man and Amanda fly from the saddle. Both hit the ground simultaneously and he heard Amanda's halfscream but he was running forward, the Colt in his hand. Amanda lay on the ground in a halfdaze as the man pushed to his feet, saw his gun on the ground some six inches from him. "Don't," Fargo said as the man started to reach for it. "Back off."

The man stopped, peered at him, hesitated, saw the Colt aimed at him but his eyes returned to the gun, so temptingly close. Then, as Fargo had seen done so often before, with that strange combination of bad judgment, bravado, and fear, the man's arm shot out for the gun. Fargo fired. . . .

THE
TRAILSMAN
#203

SILVER HOOVES

by

Jon Sharpe

A SIGNET BOOK

SIGNET
Published by the Penguin Group
Penguin Putnam Inc., 375 Hudson Street,
New York, New York 10014, U.S.A.
Penguin Books Ltd, 27 Wrights Lane,
London W8 5TZ, England
Penguin Books Australia Ltd,
Ringwood, Victoria, Australia
Penguin Books Canada Ltd, 10 Alcorn Avenue,
Toronto, Ontario, Canada M4V 3B2
Penguin Books (N.Z.) Ltd, 182–190 Wairau Road,
Auckland 10, New Zealand

Penguin Books Ltd, Registered Offices:
Harmondsworth, Middlesex, England

First published by Signet, an imprint of Dutton NAL,
a member of Penguin Putnam Inc.

First Printing, October, 1998
10 9 8 7 6 5 4 3 2 1

The first chapter of this book originally appeared in *The Stallion Search*,
the two hundred second volume in this series.

 REGISTERED TRADEMARK—MARCA REGISTRADA

Printed in the United States of America

The Trailsman

Beginnings . . . they bend the tree and they mark the man. Skye Fargo was born when he was eighteen. Terror was his midwife, vengeance his first cry. Killing spawned Skye Fargo, ruthless, cold-blooded murder. Out of the acrid smoke of gunpowder still hanging in the air, he rose, cried out a promise never forgotten.

The Trailsman they began to call him all across the West: searcher, scout, hunter, the man who could see where others only looked, his skills for hire but not his soul, the man who lived each day to the fullest, yet trailed each tomorrow. Skye Fargo, the Trailsman, and the seeker who could take the wildness of a land and the wanting of a woman and make them his own.

*1860, the New Mexico Territory,
where the southern end of the
Sangre de Cristo Mountains edged
the vast plains and looked down
on a new and deadly kind
of cattle drive . . .*

1

The big man's lake blue eyes were darkened as he scanned the jagged reaches of the Sangre de Cristo mountain range. These brutal peaks harbored a thousand ways to kill, he knew. Every crag, rock pinnacle, pointed boulder and sloping talus could bring sudden death. Every path, defile, twisting, torturous passage could plunge a horse and rider over one of the naked cliffs of sheer rock. Nature lay in wait for every intruder, ready to strike with a loose rock, an unexpected hole, a crumbling cliffside, death and danger multiplied in countless ways. And the cruel mountains were host to those who offered death in their own ways.

For the careless, sidewinders waited with their venom-filled fangs, as did the tiger rattler, the Mojave and blacktail rattler, and the coral snake, as attractive as it was deadly. For the unwary, the mountain lion could kill with one silent pounce and for the tired, the red wolf pack was relentless in pursuing its prey. In the hard, harsh mountains of the Sangre de Cristo range, humans were simply one more potential victim for the land and all its denizens of fang, claw, and talon. And now one more way for death to strike had appeared. Sky Fargo's mouth became a thin line as he scanned the sky, took in the deep purple-gray of it, the very color menacing. He ran one hand along the jet black neck of the magnificent Ovaro as the horse's ears twitched nervously, instinct signaling danger. "Easy, old friend," he murmured as his gaze swept the vast expanse of the lowering clouds.

The sky would open up soon, he knew, bursting with a fury of its own to send a deluge of water down on every crag, peak, and path in the mountains. A terrible, pounding deluge would follow and send cascades of water racing down to fill every cranny, defile, crevice, path, and road that threaded through the mountains. He had witnessed these fierce storms before, knew how they would grow in power as more and more rain poured unceasingly down onto the land. Torrents of water would consume everything in its path, dislodging sloping taluses, sending rock hurtling downward, sweeping away pieces of loose crag, and flinging more rocks in all directions. Only shelter could keep a man alive, the right shelter in the right place. He had ridden these mountains before, not often yet enough times and to him, a trail, a pathway, a passage, was forever imprinted in his mind, that special mind of a trailsman where the land was a book, a map, words and sentences made of earth, leaf, and tree. He had drawn on those imprints of nature, visualized the shelter that would keep him alive during the storm. It was one of the few places offering survival and he turned the pinto down a narrow passage, came out at the end of it on a level stretch. He rode till he recognized another short cutoff, and took it to another passage that bordered high rocks on one side, mountain brush on the other. A tall spire of granite was a remembered beacon and he rounded the path beside it. The first hard spray of rain suddenly flung itself into his face and he kept the Ovaro at a slow trot, glanced at twisted paloverde trees that somehow grew out of the mountainsides in stunted, misshapen forms. He rode on as the sky continued to fling intermittent sprays of rain at him with a kind of malicious playfulness. He'd gone perhaps another hundred yards when he caught the sound, unmistakable, and he reined to a halt, peering down over the edge of the path. The wagon raced along the narrow roadway below, one side of the road a sheer cliff, and he watched it career perilously close to the edge as it rounded a tight curve. He frowned at the rig, a closed-panel rockaway, drawn by two horses. It was no wagon for these mountains, not at any time, and now it was a rolling coffin going the wrong way in the wrong place.

He spurred the Ovaro forward, found a narrow, winding defile, and sent the horse down it until he emerged on the roadway below. He reined to a halt, peered over the edge of the sharp drop on one side, grimaced as he saw but a few hardy brush growths and the rest uneven sides of rock. The wagon came into sight moments later and he raised a hand. The wagon drew to a halt as he blocked its path and Fargo felt the furrow dig into his brow as he saw a smallish figure holding the reins, loose, dark brown hair flowing around a round-cheeked, soft face. The young woman sat motionless as he started to move closer and he saw a curtain behind her. He gestured with one hand at the sky. "You're going to get yourself killed damn soon," Fargo said. Suddenly the curtain came open and another figure pushed forward, dark brown hair worn tight and swept upward atop her head, a long, leaner face and Fargo saw the big plains rifle in the young woman's hands.

"Hell we are, damn you," the woman said as she brought up the rifle.

"Shit," Fargo swore as the shot exploded and he flung himself sideways from the saddle. He felt the shot whistle past his shoulder as he hit the ground, rolled, and stopped just at the edge of the cliffside. The Ovaro backed and Fargo glanced up to see the young woman bring the rifle around for another shot. A quick glance told him there was no place to hide and he rolled, letting himself go over the side as the second shot smashed into the rock. He fell, reached out, hit a protruding rock, managing to close his hand around a scrubby branch and halt his fall. He heard the wagon roll forward, the young woman's voice cutting through the thick, turgid air. "He was one of them. Let's get out of here," she said and Fargo heard the snap of the reins on the team, the scrape of wagon wheels on stone.

Cursing silently, he kept his grip on the length of scrub branch, using his other hand to find a crack in the rock. Slowly, he pulled himself upward, groping until he found another tiny ledge that afforded a fingerhold. He felt the branch bend as he pulled on it, paused, pulled again, and gave a sigh of relief as the branch held. Exerting a careful, steady pull, Fargo clung to the branch, lifted himself, found another tiny ledge of rock, and climbed again until he reached the edge of the roadway. He pulled one leg up, crawled over the top of the cliffside, and pushed to his feet. He found the Ovaro at once, a dozen yards away against the high rocks at one side of the road. The wagon had found the room to squeeze by and had gone on. Another spray of rain struck at Fargo as he walked to the horse.

But this time the spray was followed by a steady pelting of rain. The skies were beginning to open up, Fargo noted. Drawing his rain slicker from the saddlebag, he donned it and swinging onto the pinto, stared down the mountain road where the two young women had vanished. They'd plainly been afraid of something but the one had been too damn quick to shoot. She'd almost killed him and he'd no inclination to let her try again. He'd stopped to offer help and had damn near taken a bullet for it. The hell with them, he thought. Whatever their problems, whatever their fears, they'd have to live with them. And their own stupidity. In this case, die with them, he thought grimly. Death would most surely catch up to them. There was no hiding place, no safe refuge down the road they had taken. The area was one of cliffs, sheer drops, and granite walls with shallow overhangs that would prove to be death traps when the cascading waters began to rise and fill the narrow pathways.

He turned the Ovaro down a side passage and refused to feel guilty. You couldn't be everyone's keeper, he told himself as he increased the pinto's pace. He let the feeling of his own survival pull at him. After all, he had to reach his own refuge and that could elude him if the storm grew too fierce too quickly, rain and wind obscuring details of marks and signposts that were at best unclear. The rain had begun to come down steadily and he could feel the wind picking up speed. He peered hard through the raindrops at passing rock formations as he made his way down another passage. Suddenly he found what he sought, a narrow path that split off from the wider passage to wind up alongside a high wall of rock. Halfway up, the rock grew less severe, becoming a series of overhangs and deep indentations, scrubby trees dotting the terrain. A few hundred yards on he saw the mouth of the cave, set back from the passage and tall enough for a horse and rider to enter.

It had given him shelter once before, that time from a pursuing band of Comanches, and he steered the Ovaro into the deep, tall cave, high enough and back far enough to escape the torrent of water that would engulf the land. He dismounted and explored the cave in the light still remaining. It was relatively clean, only a few carcass bones littering the sides. Outside of the dankness common to all caves, it didn't stink of raccoon or skunk urine or the pungent odor of bear. The black bears that wandered high into the mountains preferred smaller, tighter caves for hibernation. Stepping to the mouth of the cave, he peered out at the rain that came down at a slant now, driven by new winds. The storm had strengthened, the rain drumming a tattoo against the rocks. He let another minute go by as the mixed feelings continued to churn inside him.

His lips a tight line, he turned suddenly, strode to the pinto, and pulled himself into the saddle, cursing the two young women who were victims about to happen, and himself. A conscience was a meddlesome, troublesome affliction. It made a man defy his better judgment, ignore common sense, and indulge in efforts he'd no need to take. Damn the thing, he swore as he sent the pinto out of the cave. The rain assaulted him at once and he wiped at his eyes as he peered up at the sky, estimating that he had a half hour, perhaps, before the water started down from the high peaks to race through every passageway. Keeping the horse at a slow trot, he went down the road and felt the rain increase in power. The road turned and twisted, one side high rock, the other a cliffside with a sheer drop to death far below on jagged boulders.

He kept the Ovaro against the high rock side as the road narrowed, his lips pulled back as precious minutes ticked away. He had carefully rounded a half-dozen curves when he went around the second of a pair of extremely sharp twists. As he came out of the curve he reined up sharply. The wagon rose up before him, on its side, the two horses still with it, held in place by their twisted harnesses. They pawed the ground and strained against the straps holding them, frightened, aware of death with that sixth sense all animals possess. Fargo dismounted, strode over to them, and calmed them both with his hands and voice as he peered at the overturned wagon. The rockaway lay at the very edge of the cliffside, the front almost hanging over the edge. It had plainly skidded as it took the curve too fast and went over, the front panels broken and knocked out. He stepped to the rig and peered inside. Neither of the two young women was there and he drew back, wondering if they'd fled on foot in panic. He peered at the broken panels again.

They had been knocked outward. Bodies had been flung through them when the wagon overturned. He stepped around the back of the rockaway to the edge of the cliff, squinted downward, taking a moment to adjust his vision to the rain. The narrow ledge of rock took shape some fifteen feet below him, then the two figures clinging to it. They had miraculously landed on the only ledge that jutted out of the otherwise sheer wall of rock. A few feet to the right or left and they'd have plunged to their deaths at the bottom of the drop. They lay flat on the ledge, he saw, clinging precariously, and he saw one wave up at him with one arm. Cupping his hands to his mouth, he called through the noise of the wind and rain. "Can you get up?" he asked.

The answer came back as from very far away. "It's wet and slippery." His lips drew back in a grimace. The ledge would grow wetter and more slippery the harder the rains came. When the floodwaters raced down the road they'd spill over the side and sweep the two figures from the ledge. Fargo turned, hurried to the Ovaro, and took the rope from the lariat strap. He began to wrap it around his hand as he returned to the edge of the cliff, then fashioned a noose at the other end. Dropping to one knee, he began to lower the lariat. When it reached the ledge, the smaller figure reached one arm up, grasped the rope, and pulled it to her. "Put the loop around your waist," Fargo called down. He waited as she brought the noose down to her waist. When it was in place, he pulled it tight around her. "Now hold on to the rope with both hands," he said, bracing himself against the rear of the overturned wagon.

She obeyed, bringing both hands to the rope, and he felt her slip from the ledge at once. But he was prepared, his powerful shoulder muscles tightened as the full weight of her pulled on his arms, shoulders, and back. He let her swing against the side of the cliff, hang there for a moment, and then began to pull her up. He pulled slowly, steadily, straining his back and arms. His lips drew back as he felt the rain causing his grip on the rope to slip. He heard the girl's short scream of panic as she dropped in space while he wound another turn of the rope around his hands. Starting to pull again, he felt her scraping along the face of the rock wall as he pulled her upward. She was unable to do anything but cling to the rope and hang helplessly, he realized, and he pulled harder with muscles that protested. The rain had grown stronger, hitting against him in a steady, wind-driven assault.

But finally, he saw the top of her head appear over the edge of the cliffside, then the rest of her slowly come into sight. When her shoulders reached the edge of stone, she reached out, found a finger grip, and began to pull herself onto the road. He loosened the pull on the lariat, skidded himself almost on his back, and closed one hand around her arm and helped pull her onto the road. She lay prone for a moment, drawing in deep breaths of air as he pushed onto one knee and loosened the rope from around her waist, finally pulling it free of her. Her loose, brown hair was rain-soaked but it somehow remained full around her round face. She was a smallish, compact figure, he noted briefly. "Stay right here," he told her as he went back to the end of the cliff and began to lower the lariat again.

The other young woman lay flat on the ledge, plainly not daring to move, and he maneuvered the lariat until it dropped onto her. "Take it, put it around your waist," he called. The young woman reached one hand out, brought the noose down, and began to pull it around her waist. She reached up with her other hand and as she did, her feet slipped on the wet rock.

He yanked hard to close the noose as she went over the edge with a scream, the feel of her sudden weight pulling against his arms. "Damn," he spit out as he slid forward on the wet stone, his body only inches from the edge. Keeping his grip on the rope, he rolled, and holding his arms over his head, found a few inches more as the road curved and managed to get one heel up against a small rise of stone. It was enough to keep him from being pulled over the edge as he pushed hard against it, sweat mingling with the rain coursing down his face.

He rested a moment, took in a deep breath, and felt the figure swinging in the air at the other end of the rope. He felt for the young woman's panic, unable to do anything but hang helplessly in midair. Slowly, he gathered his strength again and began to pull. He cursed at the rain that continued to make his grip on the rope slip. Casting a quick glance at the young woman who sat against the wagon, he saw that she was frozen in place, staring with her eyes wide. "Get over here," Fargo shouted. His sharp cry snapped the half trance and she blinked, swung herself around, and crawled to him. "Take a hold and pull, dammit," he rasped and she grasped the lariat a few inches in front of his hands. "Every little bit helps," he muttered as his muscles cried out again as he took a long pull. Looking at the rope where it scraped against the edge of the cliffside, he was grateful to see it had not frayed yet.

Though time passed as usual, it seemed made of lead as the girl pulled with him and he was glad for what little she contributed. His arms seemed ready to pull out of their shoulder sockets when the young woman's head appeared, then her shoulders. "Give her a hand," Fargo ordered. Finding a reservoir of strength in his straining muscles, he leaned back in order to keep the rope taut. The girl crawled to the edge of the cliff, lying flat as she reached out with both arms and closed hands around her friend's shoulders. She pulled as the other young woman drew one leg up and half pushed herself onto the top of the road and safety. Fargo let the lariat go limp and heaved a deep breath of his own. He moved to the young woman, who lay prone beside the wagon, loosened the noose, and lifted it from her as she looked up at him, gratitude flooding her face.

A long, thin face, not at all like the other girl's, Fargo noted as he extended a hand, helping her to her feet. She was a lot taller than the other girl, her figure lean, her hair swept up atop her head, as he had seen when he glimpsed her in the wagon. The heavy rain made a good look at her impossible and he straightened, his voice hard. "Let's go. We're on borrowed time," he said. "Unhitch the horses. You'll be riding them."

"Get our bags," the taller girl said to the other as she strode to the horses and began to undo the harness and reins. Fargo went to the Ovaro and swung onto the saddle as the round-faced girl came from the wagon carrying two leather traveling bags.

"You ever ride bareback?" Fargo asked them both.

"Yes," the tall one said and the other nodded agreement.

"This time you'll be riding wet on a wet horse. We'll stay at a walk," Fargo said. "We've no time to have you sliding off every few minutes." He watched both young women pull themselves onto the horses, each with a bag slung over one shoulder. They managed to mount without problems, and came alongside him as he sent the Ovaro back down the road. At least two inches of water now coursed atop the road, he saw, and cursed silently. The two inches would soon be six feet of racing water, pushed by thousands of pounds of force from the high peaks, made even more powerful as it channeled through narrow passages. Fargo shot a rainswept glance at the sky. Daylight still clung but it was a dark, threatening, glowering daylight and Fargo forced himself to keep the pinto at a walk. The rain bounced from his rain slicker and as he shot a glance at the two young women, he saw the round-faced one shiver as she rode. Fargo made his way back the way he had come and when he reached the road that turned off upward to the cave, the water flowed ankle-deep against the pinto's legs.

Fargo led the way up the narrow incline to the cave, and rode into the high-ceilinged shelter. He swung from the saddle as the two young women followed him in. He pulled his rain slicker off as the two women slid from their horses and he had a chance to properly look at them for the first time. The smaller, round-faced one had a soft prettiness to her, even soaked as she was. Her blouse clung to high breasts that somehow echoed the roundness of her face, two little points pushing sharply into the wet fabric. Dark brown eyes gazed back at him from a pretty, almost babyish face, full lips adding to the picture.

His glance went to the other young woman. She had none of the round-faced prettiness of the first one, her face long and angular with a straight nose and almost prim mouth. Yet there was a strong attractiveness in it, high cheekbones giving her a chiseled imperiousness. Her soaked blouse also rested against her breasts, but these were long, slow-curving mounds that fitted the rest of her lean, narrow body, torso, hips, legs, all of flowing symmetry. Only the cool severity of her marred what might be a patrician kind of beauty, he decided. The round-cheeked one spoke up first. "We're soaked to the skin and cold. We've dry clothes in our bags. We want to change," she said.

"Go ahead," he grunted.

"We're not inclined to put on a show," the tall one said.

"Go back deep into the cave. It'll be too dark there for me to see you," he said.

They nodded in unison and he watched them go to their traveling bags and take out towels and dry clothes. They walked together back into the interior of the cave, where they faded away in the darkness where no daylight penetrated. He went to the mouth of the cave and stared out at the water rushing past on the road below, already nearing four feet in height. He watched it churn, spit foam, and bubble and he turned only when he heard the sound behind him. Both young women stood before him in dry clothes, peering at him, the round-faced one with open curiosity, the tall, lean one with severity. She spoke first, this time. "Why'd you come back?" she asked.

"Because I'm not whoever the hell you thought I was, honey," he tossed back. "And I've a conscience that makes me protect damn fools." He turned, strode to the edge of the cave entrance, and motioned to them. They came and halted beside him, their eyes widening as they stared down at the rushing torrent of water that had risen another foot higher. "That's where you'd be, swept away in that, and it's going to get worse," he said. "If you hadn't skidded and overturned you'd be swept away and drowning by now."

The smaller one swallowed hard and stepped back as a gust of wind pelted her with rain. Her eyes fastened on him. "Thank God for your conscience," she murmured. He stepped back and she went with him as the taller one followed. "I'm Angela Carter. This is my sister, Amanda. You can be surprised. Everybody is. We don't look like sisters."

"I'm not surprised," Fargo said and she raised an eyebrow. "I've seen that before with sisters," he finished. "I'm Fargo . . . Skye Fargo. Some people call me the Trailsman. Now, you want to tell me what you were doing in a rockaway up in these mountains?"

"Trying to take a shortcut down to the plains east of here instead of going the long way around," Angela said.

"Damn fools. I'll say it again," Fargo snapped. "That's no rig for these mountains. No wonder it went over at the first chance."

"We thought it'd be faster than a heavy mountain wagon," Angela said.

Fargo's lake blue eyes wore a coating of frost as he turned them on Amanda. "That doesn't explain why you took two shots at me," he growled.

"I thought you were trying to stop us," Amanda said.

"From going through the mountains?" He frowned.

"From reaching our herd on the plains," she answered.

Fargo's frown stayed as he sat down on the floor of the cave. Angela quickly followed suit, folding her compact figure down across from him, her soft, round

22

face warm and open. Amanda stayed standing, cool, contained appraisal in her face, and Fargo found himself wondering how two pairs of brown eyes could be so different. "I think you'd better start at the beginning," he said.

2

Angela glanced at Amanda, a silent, private exchange. Had her eyes asked permission, Fargo wondered, and decided she'd asked approval more than permission, her soft, round face not without its own brand of determination. "Amanda and I have a cattle ranch," she said.

Fargo stared back. "You don't seem like cattle ranchers," he said, his glance lingering on Angela. "Sure as hell not you."

Angela gave an almost sheepish smile. "Looks are deceiving. But you're half right. I do mostly managing and bookkeeping. Amanda does the real ranching. The place belonged to our pa. He died not long ago, left it all to us. Luckily, Amanda had always taken more interest in the operation than I did." Fargo glanced at Amanda and found it easy to accept Angela's words. "We run mostly whiteface," she said, "Herefords to use their correct name. We don't like longhorns. A lot of the ranchers around here don't. They pretty much all say that. They're mean, stubborn, and short-tempered."

Amanda cut in. "Coarse-headed, coarse-haired, slab-sided, thin-flanked, three-quarters horn and hooves and the rest hair," she said.

"Heard that before about them." Fargo smiled.

"We send our Herefords east, across the upper strip of the Oklahoma Territory, then north into Kansas to Dodge City or sometimes Wichita," Amanda said. "But there's been trouble lately. Ed Steiner's herd was attacked, all his cowhands killed. Same with Frank Callum's herd. Angela and I stayed at the ranch and let our foreman take this herd through. Then we heard that somebody planned an attack on it."

"I'd hired almost all new hands," Angela said. "When word came to us, we took off to get to our herd and warn everyone."

"The shortcut through the mountains," Fargo said and Angela nodded.

"When you cut us off on the road, we thought you were one of those trying to stop us," Angela said.

"Why didn't you ride? Why take the rockaway?" Fargo asked.

"We were bringing two cases of extra rifles and ammo," Amanda said.

"They'll be smashed at the bottom of some ravine along with your wagon," Fargo said.

Angela cast a glance at the mouth of the cave. "So now we've no choice but to wait till the storm passes and then go on. We want to reach the herd," she said.

Fargo's thoughts leapfrogged and he decided there was nothing to be gained by holding them back. "This storm will last through the night, I'd guess. The prairie will be soaked through. It's soft ground to begin with. It'll become one huge mudhole. I hope your cowhands are experienced."

"Not very, I'd guess. They're young. Why?"

"They don't spread out the herd before the storm hit, you're in real trouble," Fargo said.

"How?" She frowned.

"A herd kept together sinks together. When the ground softens enough, their combined weight in one place will suck them right down, fast and deep, too deep for them to get out. I've seen cattle mired up to their necks."

Angela rose, twisting her hands together. "Good God," she muttered. "How awful. Maybe they spread the herd out. Maybe they knew enough."

"You'll find out when the storm's over in the morning," Fargo said and she turned, strode to the cave entrance, and stared out at the pouring rain and the racing waters that now swept by but a few feet from the cave. He rose, went to stand beside her, and saw the day quickly coming to an end. Suddenly her hand was holding his arm and she pressed against him.

"Except for you, we'd be in there. Thank you, Fargo, for coming back." Amanda came up and Fargo felt her disapproval as she halted beside them.

"I'll see if I can get a fire going," he said and returned to the inside of the tall cave. He scoured the edges, found enough old, dry pieces of tree branches undoubtedly dragged in by some animal. When he got a small fire going, Angela and Amanda joined him around the flame as the storm winds whistled outside and the racing waters were a terrifying obligato. They sat in silence until Angela rose, went to her travel bag, and returned with strips of dried beef. He took one at Angela's offer, ate in silence with the two young women. They were a study in contrasts, he pondered. Not only in looks, in basic personalities, attitudes, probably in everything. Certainly in outer warmth.

Sometimes contrasts got along famously, complementing each other. He wondered if that was the case with Amanda and Angela. But sometimes contrasts meant underground tensions and conflicts. He wondered about these two, even as he knew it was an exercise in idle speculation. He had saved their lives, a passing good deed. He'd no time to do more for them. As the fire began to die out, Angela rose and came to him. "I'm taking my blanket as far back in the cave as I can, where I won't hear that damn water," she said. Stepping forward, she reached up, pulled his face down to hers, and her full lips were soft and pliable. "Thank you, again, Skye Fargo," she murmured, turned, and hurried away, her round, high breasts gently bouncing.

Amanda stayed unmoving until Angela disappeared into the blackness at the rear of the cave. She rose then, unfolding her long figure. The remains of the fire cast a fitful light that flickered on the long curve of her breasts and the length of one thigh. Her eyes held on him, her face unsmiling. "I'm not ungrateful for what you did, Fargo," she said.

He smiled. "You just have trouble saying it," he answered.

"Angela is the demonstrative one," she said.

"By default?" he asked.

She allowed a half shrug. "One of us has to hold back on being impulsive. I protect her from herself. I promised Father I'd do that."

"I think it's a promise you enjoy keeping," he pushed at her and saw her eyes narrow at him. "I'm

27

wondering if you're protecting her from herself or you from yourself."

"That's impertinent," she flared.

"I'm full of bad habits." He laughed.

"Good night," she said coldly as she brushed past him to also disappear into the rear of the cave. He went to the cave entrance, peered out at the torrent of rushing water. It hadn't risen any higher but it hadn't lost any force, either. It was a storm to turn the flatlands below into a quagmire. He could have only misgivings for what they'd find when they reached the plains. He unsaddled the pinto, took his sleeping roll, and set it out, undressed, and lay down as the last of the fire flickered out. The sound of the rushing water became an ominous lullaby that finally put him to sleep.

The morning was still gray when he woke, clouds still curtaining away the new day's sun. He rose, took a towel from his saddlebag, and naked, stepped outside where the rain still fell, but a light drizzle now, and he washed, stepped back into the cave, and dried himself. He'd just drawn on jeans when Angela and Amanda appeared, both dressed. He gestured to the light rain. "Shower?" he asked. "Courtesy of God."

"Ogling, courtesy of Fargo," Amanda said. "We'll wait till we get to a town and a hotel."

He finished dressing as the rain stopped and he gazed at the roadway below. Some ten inches of water still coursed down the path. It would stay that way until the last of it came down from the high peaks runoff, not enough to prevent their riding but enough to dictate caution. "Get your horses. We'll keep at a walk," he said.

"All the way down?" Angela asked.

"If you want to get there in one piece," Fargo said and swung onto the pinto, guided the horse out onto the water-covered path. Angela came up to ride beside him, Amanda staying behind them. He moved carefully through the passages, all still carrying water in varying depths. In the narrow defiles, they rode single file and as they neared the base of the range, the passages grew wider. Angela came up to ride beside him again. He saw nervous apprehension in her face and she threw quick glances at him, as if looking for reassurance. But he kept his face impassive, unwilling to offer what he had no right to offer. He was first onto the flatland where the mountains ended and he immediately felt the water-soaked land's sucking pull on the Ovaro's hooves. Amanda came up to ride beside him, Angela at his other side, and Fargo moved slowly over the prairie, all too aware that the soft, sucking mud could twist a horse's ankle with deceptive ease.

The land stretched out and Fargo's eyes noted the wide patches where water lay across the surface, ground so soft it would collapse under even a man's footsteps and become an instant, giant sinkhole. The rain stopped but the grayness still held the sky as the three riders moved over the prairie, Fargo pointing out the danger spots, leading the others in winding, time-consuming circles. They had ridden most of the morning when Fargo saw the objects rise up on the horizon, his quick glance at Angela telling him she had seen them also. She immediately put her horse into a trot. "Slow down," Fargo barked as he saw the horse's feet skid instantly on the treacherous ground. With its own instinctive awareness, her horse balked, ignored her urging and fought the reins and she was forced to slow down. "Horse sense," Fargo muttered as he returned his gaze to the horizon as he plodded forward.

The objects began to slowly take shape, partly becoming visible mounds of brown fur. "Oh my God, oh my God," Angela cried out as she tried to rush her horse forward again but Fargo reached out, yanking back on her reins as the horse slipped and managed to recover.

"Slow, dammit," he said, and held her at a walk as he went forward. The objects grew closer and Fargo's eyes swept the scene as his lips pulled back in a grimace. The entire herd, bunched together, were imbedded in the ground, some sunk down with only their heads showing, others with their upper bodies still visible but just as helpless. Some were lying on their sides, no longer breathing as the others emitted hoarse, bellowing sounds. The earth had caved in below them, pulling them down in a giant sinkhole that immediately engulfed them, surrounding them with thick, clinging, heavy mud. In moments, they had become victims of the storm and the earth, rendered helpless. The more they fought the more they dug themselves in until, with inexorable power, the mud-soaked earth claimed its deadly victory.

He dismounted, Angela's voice a mixture of sobs and curses in his ear as he walked to the edge of the circular hole and the brown mounds of fur and horn. He swore inwardly and lifting his eyes, he saw Angela and Amanda had dismounted and were standing at the edge of the circle, shock and horror in both their faces. Fargo's eyes moved to the other forms that lay just beyond the giant mudhole. He counted eight as he walked to the silent, prone figures and felt the frown slide across his brow. He looked up as Amanda came up, following his stare. He knelt down on one knee as he peered at the nearest figure, then the next, rose, and went to each prone, silent form. Finally he rose and turned to Amanda.

"The storm didn't kill your hands. Bullets did," he said. "A fast attack, I'd say. They were hit while they were trying to save some of the herd. Some still have lariats attached to steers."

"Yes, I see," Amanda said, shock in her voice.

"How awful. God, how awful," Angela said but Fargo's eyes had turned to the remains of two wagons that lay nearby.

"They yours?" he asked.

"Yes, one's the chuck wagon," Amanda said.

"The other?"

"Supply wagon. We always send a supply wagon with every drive," she said.

Fargo strode to the chuck wagon and peered at the wreckage as the frown dug deeper into his brow. "It's been completely torn apart," he said as Amanda and Angela came up. "Look here, they not only tore apart the wagon, they even went through the possum belly, the wreck pan, and the squirrel can. They went over the chuck wagon with a fine-tooth comb." He turned to the supply wagon, pointed out the floor-boards torn up, axles and wheels smashed open. "Why? What were they looking for? Why'd they tear up a chuck wagon and smash open a supply wagon?" Angela and Amanda shrugged in unison. "I wonder if they were interested in the herd," Fargo thought aloud.

"Of course they were. That's what they came for. When they got here they found the herd in the pit. They were so mad they just went on a killing and wrecking spree," Angela said.

He let his lips purse in thought. "It's possible, but it doesn't make much sense," Fargo said.

"Being frustrated isn't about making sense," Angela said. "They drove off with Ed Steiner's steers. Bob Callum's herd, too. They were just crazy mad they couldn't get ours." He didn't argue further. He'd nothing concrete to offer her but the unsatisfied feeling stayed inside him. Something just didn't sit right. "What about the wagons?" Angela asked, breaking into his thoughts. "What about our steers? Can we save them?"

"Some are already gone. You'd need twenty men and a block and tackle for the rest," Fargo said and hated how coldly cruel he sounded.

"We just leave them like this? What'll happen to them?" Angela protested.

"First wolves, coyotes, bears, cougars, and vultures. They'll all have a free meal. Then the carrion beetles, millepedes, springtails, and worms, all of nature's housecleaners. They'll finish the job."

"They'll eat our helpless steers alive? No, it's too awful," Angela said.

"Then we do the only thing to do," Fargo said. Angela stared, a frown creasing her brow. Fargo drew the big Henry from its saddlecase. "It's the only humane thing to do," he said.

Angela stared back, horror in her eyes. Amanda's voice broke the silence. "It's terrible, but he's right. It'll be less cruel than leaving them to an awful death," she said.

Fargo offered her the rifle. "You want to do it? They're your steers."

Amanda turned away, her patrician profile beautifully stark. "No," she murmured. "You do it. Please."

He nodded and turned away. You learn things in unexpected ways, he reminded himself. Her contained coolness didn't go very deep. He walked away, raised the rifle, and fired the first shot and grimaced. The grimace stayed as he slowly walked around the herd, taking careful aim at one steer after the other, cursing the task. An act of mercy, the humane thing, the only thing to do, an exercise in compassion, all of it absolutely true and none of it enough to prevent the sour distaste that curdled inside him. He had half finished the job when Angela's cry cut through the air.

"No, no more. Stop," she burst out and he lowered the rifle, meeting her eyes as she came forward. "I want to wait," she said.

"For what?" Fargo questioned. "Nothing's changed."

"Maybe it will," Angela said. "Maybe after the ground dries, some can pull themselves out."

"When the ground hardens they'll be packed in even tighter," Fargo said and saw her full lips grow thin, adamancy sliding across her face.

"Maybe not, maybe not," Angela insisted. "Maybe some will have a chance. No more killing until they have that. No more. They stay till tomorrow. Then we'll see."

"They won't have a tomorrow," Fargo told her, shooting a glance at Amanda. It asked for support.

"I don't know what to think," she said helplessly.

"I want to wait. No more killing until tomorrow, no

more," Angela said. Fargo heard her voice rise, a strident adamancy spiraling in it. There was no way to argue with her, he saw. She rejected reality and reason, humanity and logic. She was caught in the web of her own emotions. "We'll go to Almeda, spend the night there," she said to Amanda and strode to her horse.

Fargo saw Amanda's eyes go to him as she shrugged. "You can't reach her when she's this way. Angela's soft inside as well as outside. She's always been unable to face trouble, life, reality, Pa knew that. It's why he made me promise to take care of her. She gets caught up in her own emotions and there's no reasoning with her."

"Sounds as if she finds her own strength when she wants to," Fargo said.

"No. The softness and compassion inside her just overwhelms her," Amanda said. "She gets carried away." She turned to her horse and paused. "Ride to Almeda with us," she said.

"I'll ride partway with you," Fargo said and pulled himself onto the Ovaro, returned the rifle to its case, and cast a glance at Amanda as he swung the pinto beside her. She appeared to understand Angela yet her severely lovely face showed more disapproval than understanding. Maybe the two could go together, he debated silently. Angela moved her horse forward as they came alongside where she waited and they rode in silence, Angela's face still showing her inner tension. The day was starting to draw to an end when he reined up. "I'll be leaving you, now," Fargo said.

Amanda turned to him. "I thought you might like to work for us. We'll be needing more hands and you're a trailsman," she said.

"Sorry, got a job waiting. Man sent me an advance," Fargo said.

"We'll double it," Amanda said.

"That's not right, Amanda," Angela cut in. "You wouldn't like it done to you."

"It's been done to me. It's Fargo's call," Amanda said.

"I made a promise. I keep my word," Fargo said. "You might even know the man. He's not that far from here. Frank Bannister."

"Bannister Silver Mine?" Angela said.

"That's right," Fargo nodded.

"What's he want with you?" Angela frowned.

"Don't know yet," Fargo said.

"If it doesn't work out, come see us," Amanda said. "We're directly north of Almeda."

Angela suddenly moved her horse, came around to the other side of Fargo, leaned from the saddle, and kissed him, a sudden, quick gesture. "For everything," she said, pulling her soft lips back and riding away.

"Impulsive." Amanda sniffed and rode after her sister. Fargo put the pinto into a trot and turned south. Frank Bannister's instructions said that his place was southwest of Almeda, but Fargo saw the night lowering and decided not to try and reach it. He put distance between himself and the grim, grisly scene behind him, riding until he spied three sycamores leaning on each other. He halted beneath them as night fell, unsaddled the Ovaro, and sat down on the ground, which was just beginning to harden. Coolness came with the night and he set out his sleeping bag, sat beside it, and chewed a stick of beef jerky. Leaning back against the mottled cream color bark of the sycamore, he watched the stars appear and the almost full moon start its upward climb. He felt himself slowly relax, his first thoughts on the massacre returning to him, the wagons torn apart, the cowhands gunned down.

Angela's explanation of frustration and fury still refused to sit right with him. It had been a strange attack for which he had no explanation. Yet there had to be another one, he told himself. But he could come up with none that satisfied and finally he turned off the fruitless speculation, shed clothes, and slid into his bedroll. The moon had risen high, bathing the prairie in its pale light. It took him a while to completely turn off his churning thoughts and he had just begun to doze off when he heard the sound, distant and dim, a soft popping noise, almost like children puncturing balloons.

He sat up, suddenly fully alert. No balloons popping, he frowned after another moment, the sounds taking on new character. "Rifle fire," he muttered, in the distance. He pushed from the bedroll and pulled on his clothes. The shots grew faster, a sudden franticness to them. He ran to the Ovaro, but decided that putting on the saddle would take too much time. He yanked the rifle from its case, grabbed the extra ammunition belt, and vaulted onto the horse's back. The Ovaro, always in tune with its rider, broke into a gallop immediately. Fargo raced into the moonlit night, followed the sound, and soon cursed as he saw where he was headed. The pit came into view and now he heard the other sounds, snarls and growls, half barks and the furious clashing of fangs. The sounds became shapes, racing back and forth, leaping atop the slain steers, diving down from their fallen prey. He found the compact figure, on one knee, reloading the rifle as a wolf pack circled her, loose brown hair framing the soft face now tight with fear.

Reining to a halt, Fargo dropped from the pinto, firing as he hit the ground. His first shot caught a big red form in the middle of a leap and the animal somersaulted in midair as it went down. His next shots brought down two wolves darting at Angela from behind her and he swung the rifle, firing off another volley. The pack scattered and raced away, some leaping down into the pit. He peered across to the other side, where more wolves and at least three bears were tearing at the steer flesh. He turned to Angela. "What the hell are you doing here?" he flung at her.

She gathered herself before answering. "I decided I couldn't leave them to be eaten alive," she said.

"Where's Amanda?" he questioned.

"Back at the inn, asleep."

"Why?"

"Didn't tell her I was going. She'd only have argued me out of it."

"She'd have been right," Fargo growled. "Where'd you get the rifle?"

"Bought it in town," Angela said. He broke off further talk as he spotted some seven or eight wolves advancing from the left. Raising the Henry, he fired off a fast volley and saw them retreat at once. He turned his eyes back to Angela.

"Why, dammit?" he snapped.

"I couldn't sleep, decided I could scare at least some of them away. It was working, at first, then more came, especially the wolves. They came at me. They wouldn't scare, wouldn't back off," Angela said.

"Of course not. They had a banquet spread out in front of them," Fargo said. He rose and pulled her to her feet. "Get your horse. You can't do anything here except get yourself killed." He strode to the Ovaro as Angela climbed onto her horse, the sounds of growls and crunching jaws growing louder behind him. She swung beside him as he put the Ovaro into a fast trot, keeping an eye on two wolf packs that started to chase after them until they broke off to return to their free meal. He slowed, then rode to where he'd left his saddle and bedroll under the sycamores and reined to a halt and dismounted. Angela swung down from her horse. She stared at the saddle and his bedroll.

"I've been wondering how you happened to come after me," she said. "You were camped here, heard the shots."

"Bull's-eye," Fargo said.

She came to him and put both hands against his chest. "They were closing in on me. They'd have had me if you hadn't come. That makes the second time you've saved my life," she said. Her hands slid upward, came around his neck, and her lips touched his, warm and soft. They stayed, this time, soft pressure, until she finally pulled away. "I don't want to go back to the inn, not yet," she said, her arms staying around his neck as she pulled him onto the bedroll with her. He peered into her brown eyes, now suddenly narrowed and smoldering.

"Gratitude?" he asked.

"Partly," she said.

"What else?" he questioned.

She gave a half shrug. "Amanda says I'm impulsive."

"She's right, I'm thinking," Fargo said.

"You disapprove?"

"Hell, no," Fargo said. Her lips came to him again, her tongue darting forward, touching, then drawing back. He pressed harder, letting his own tongue answer, and her lips parted, responded.

"Yes," she murmured. "Oh, yes." She lay back on the bedroll, one hand unbuttoning the blouse until it fell open. With a wriggle, she shook it off and he took in high, very round breasts, modest yet terribly beautiful, twin mounds perfectly formed, each tipped by a tiny, almost flat nipple. She pushed down her skirt as he shed his clothes and he saw a round, almost barrel rib cage, a fleshy waist, and below it, a convex little belly, deliciously rounded. Curving downward, smooth skin carried a tiny fold over the Venus mound, adorned by a thick, bushy, very black triangle. Well-covered thighs with very round knees echoed the rest of her body, everything softness, an almost adolescent quality to her.

She turned to him and arched her back, bringing her very round breasts upward to touch his lips. He closed his mouth around one, and drawing in the softness of it, he could feel it push in at his touch. "Ah . . . aaaah," Angela purred as he slowly caressed the flat tip with his tongue, causing it to rise and push upward almost shyly. He caressed gently and Angela's torso half twisted, rounded hips lifting. His hand moved down across the barreled rib cage, slowly tracing an invisible path and moving down to the deliciously round little belly, where he paused at the little indentation. Bringing his lips to her other breast, he sucked gently on the twin mound as his hand slid downward, pressing the little fold of skin that brought him to her pubic mound. He pressed gently on the little hummock and found no wiry bushiness. Even her bushy triangle had a lanuginous softness to it as he ran his fingers into it, another echo of the softness of her. "Oh, God . . . oh, oh," he heard Angela murmur as his hand crept lower and suddenly she gave a tiny spasm and her hand flew down and came over his.

He halted. She trembled, held his hand, and then slowly pushed against it. She half turned, her mouth finding his, working hungrily against him. Half-murmured sounds came from her as his hand came down to her inner thighs, to the dampness of her, an exciting sensation. "Please, please . . . oh, God, please," Angela whispered hoarsely and he touched the tip of the dark, moist portal. She gave a gasp, then another, and he touched the roscid softness. Pressing between her soft thighs, he explored deeper, and Angela's gasp became a half cry wreathed in pleasure. Her hands dug into his shoulders as her torso lifted, fell back, and pushed forward. He explored deeper, caressing the soft, moist walls as she cried out, short, high-pitched little cries, each filled with urging.

Suddenly she turned and her compact body was all over him, pushing against him, clasping, clutching, flesh urging flesh. Little gasped cries fell from her lips and she was all softness as his throbbing maleness rose to come against her. She screamed at the touch, pressing her warm little belly against him, the cushiony padding enveloped him, and then she drew back and slid against him, seeking, wanting. He pushed upward, holding her as he found the warm wetness of her and slid slowly into the honeyed tunnel. Angela screamed, the sound of pure ecstasy spiraling into the night, as her fleshy thighs came tight against him. "Oh, yes, yes, yes," she murmured between gasps, quickly falling into a delicious rhythm with his slow thrustings, each gasped cry matching each motion, bodies suddenly as one. She pressed her soft breasts into him, the sweet pillows almost flattening against his face, and the murmured sounds from her grew low, purring, and throaty.

She felt wonderfully warm around him, both soothing and exciting at once, and he felt her flowing over him, lubricant of passion, fluid of sensuousness. With a seeming will of its own, his body asserted control, the dominance of the senses carrying him along on currents he could neither deny nor halt. The spiral rose and grew higher and higher as Angela's voice screamed out short, staccato cries of ecstasy. She clasped tighter to him and suddenly the sweet rage exploded and he heard himself cry out with her as she trembled, clinging to him and crying out in the anguish of absolute pleasure. Finally, in the seconds that seemed eternal, he was sinking down with her, murmuring in the warm aftermath of sensory embers. "Stay, stay . . ." she whispered, as though he could do any less as he reveled in the soft contractions of her that still closed around him. When she ceased her small sighs of contentment, she pushed up on one elbow, her round breasts swaying beautifully. She peered at him with a half smile edging her lips.

"That was big-time impulsive," he remarked.

"Your fault," she flipped back and he let a raised eyebrow question. "You bring out the best in a girl. Or maybe the worst," she said.

"I'll go with the best," he answered. "But I'm wondering."

"What?"

"How much you share with Amanda."

"Not this. She'd have a cat fit. She'd never understand," Angela said.

"She's protective of you," Fargo said.

"Is she?" Angela returned and he caught the edge in the remark.

"What else?" he asked.

"She's jealous of me," Angela said. "Of the way people take to me. Impulsive? Maybe but I'd rather be the way I am than like her, all held in, always holding back."

"Maybe she just cares about you," Fargo tried.

"There's caring and there's cold," Angela returned and he grimaced inwardly. She was echoing the thought that had flickered in his mind. But from her it sounded somehow ungrateful.

"Any kind of caring means something," he said and realized the weakness of the answer. She returned only skeptical silence and lay down beside him. In moments she was asleep against him and he frowned at her as he decided she was a strange mixture, apparently far more complex than Amanda. He held her inside the sleeping bag and closed his eyes, letting sleep take over. He woke when he felt her sit up. He saw the moon at the horizon line though the night was still dark.

"I want to get back before Amanda wakes," Angela said, pulling on her blouse.

"I'll ride with you," he said and began to gather his clothes.

"That'd be nice," she said and when they were both dressed she came to him, arms encircling his neck. "You've done so much, especially for me. I want you to finish your job, forget about us till you're done, then come see me. I'll make up for lost time, promise."

"I'll take you up on that," he said and she swung onto her horse as he climbed onto the Ovaro. "What do you figure to do now?" he asked as they rode.

"Hire new hands and get ready for another drive. We've plenty of steers left. We'll be all right," she said and he wished he could share her confidence. All the bothersome things about the raid still poked at him. The trip wasn't too long and they reached the silent, sleeping town with the first light of day. She halted outside the inn, dismounted, and blew him a kiss.

"Take care of yourself. Same for Amanda," Fargo said.

"We will," Angela said and hurried into the inn. He turned the pinto and moved at a walk through the wide main street of Almeda, a lone rider in the deserted thoroughfare. Almeda was pretty much as he remembered it, he noted, the same shops, the same rickety warehouses, a new barber pole. The saloon, closed and dark, bore the same name on the wood sign over the front doors: TEQUILA NOCHES. It boasted the best tequila, the best food, and the best girls and did pretty well on its boast. He wondered if the same madam still ran the place and recalled her name after a moment's search of his memory. "Juanita," he breathed aloud, seeing her in his mind, full-figured with sharp, black eyes and shiny black hair, a definite trace of Mexican blood in her broad, flat face. The saloon was owned by a man who'd added gambling to the food, girls, and booze, Fargo remembered. Drawing on his memory again, he found the man's name—Clyde Keyser, and recalled a man who took sharpness to the edge of oiliness and favored flowered vests and fancy clothes

As Fargo left the town, the first pink streaks of dawn painted the sky and he turned the pinto south and put aside thoughts of Almeda. Putting aside thoughts of Angela would take more effort, he realized as he rode across the prairie.

3

The hot sun helped to quickly dry the land as he skirted the southern tip of the Sangre de Cristo range and followed the instructions Frank Bannister had sent him. He had ridden through the morning when he saw the promontory jut out from the mountains, long and high as it poked into the flatland. As he drew closer, half a dozen buildings appeared, clustered at the edge of the mountain. Long, wooden chutes took shape, along with corrals and a collection of heavy haulage wagons with full platform gears under their sturdy bodies. He saw men coming out of the mountain pushing wheelbarrows filled with ore as he rode to a halt in front of a building less of a shack than the others with the word OFFICE over the door.

As he dismounted, a man hurried from the building and came toward him, medium height with graying hair and a square, clean-shaven face. "Skye Fargo," he called out.

"That's right," Fargo said with some surprise. "You make lucky guesses all the time?"

"Wish I did." The man laughed. "Ed Denton told me you rode a handsome Ovaro."

"Then you must be Frank Bannister," Fargo said and took the man's extended hand.

"Come inside. Don't like talking under a hot sun," Frank Bannister said and Fargo followed the man into the building. He found himself in a large office where a battered desk and file cabinets took up one half of the room, mining tools the other half. He slid his long frame into a heavy wood chair as Frank Bannister sat down across from him and began to talk with no polite preliminaries. "I sent for you because you're sort of my last hope, Fargo," he began. "Ed Denton and some others told me that if there's a trail that can be found you can find it."

"I'm good and I'm thorough. I'm also lucky." Fargo smiled. "You need all three to be a good trailsman."

"You will for this. Every one of my last four shipments have been hijacked, attacked, my men killed, my wagons run off. Each shipment was worth maybe fifty thousand in silver. I can't hire a crew anymore. Men are afraid to work for me. But the killing and the hijacking are only part of it. Somehow, my silver is getting all the way to Dodge City. I know because I'm the only miner supplying silver to Dodge and Wichita. It has to be my silver."

Fargo let his lips purse as he spoke. "That's a long way to haul all that ore without being caught." He frowned.

"You're goddamn right," Bannister said, pounding one fist on the desktop. "But they're getting it through. Somehow, someway, they're getting it through and right under my nose. I've had men stopping every damn thing that moves, searching wagon trains, freight rigs, single wagons, even individual riders, everything that crossed the prairies. They haven't found a damn thing."

"There's a lot of prairie to cover," Fargo said.

"Yes, but there's not a lot of places to hide, either."

"I suppose you've had people out searching by night," Fargo said.

"Night, day, every damn time you can think of. Sure, we could've missed a wagon or two at night but we didn't find a one. I sent for you because I hope you can pick up something my people have missed, a trail, a sign, a mark, the things they say you see that other people don't," Bannister said.

"I'd guess it's no secret that your silver shipments have been hijacked," Fargo said. "Which means you're not the only ones out searching."

"I'm sure others have been trying to get their hands on all that silver. But they haven't. Word would've gotten around if they had," Bannister said.

"Most likely," Fargo agreed. "But there are others. That likely explains the strange raid on a cattle drive. Angela and Amanda Carter's herd. I understand you know them."

"Yes, knew their pa," the man said.

"A gang raided their drive, massacred all their hands, and tore apart their two wagons but ignored the herd, most of it mired in a sinkhole. Angela thinks they tore apart the wagons out of frustration but I wonder even more now."

Bannister's brow wrinkled in a deep frown. "Yes, they raided Ed Steiner's herd, Bob Callum's, too. Tore apart their wagons, too, I heard."

"Somebody figured a cattle drive was a clever cover to get the silver through," Fargo said.

"Only they were wrong. They didn't get anything. Still it would've made a smart cover, I'll admit. I never thought of it because Ed and Bob and the Carter

47

girls are all friends of mine," Bannister said. "But there's one more thing I have to tell you. I can't figure the answer to that either and it makes everything worse."

"How's that?" Fargo inquired.

"We ship our silver still in the ore. To extract silver from its base ore, mostly argentite, you need a big smeltering operation or the giant pounders that crush the ore so the silver can be separated. We let the buyers handle that. We get less money for silver delivered in its ore but it's still a handsome profit and less work for us. But word has it that the silver reaching Dodge and Wichita is already extracted."

"Making it much smaller and easier to smuggle through," Fargo said.

"Exactly, and I can't figure how the hell they're extracting it," Bannister said.

"In the mountains back of you?" Fargo suggested.

"There's no smelter up there and if they're using the pounders you can hear them for miles. We'd have heard them for sure," Bannister said.

Fargo rose and Bannister followed him out of the shack, waiting as Fargo's eyes squinted as they scanned the vastness of the prairie and the abrupt rise of the mountain range. "I'll give it my best," he said. "Where were your shipments hijacked?"

"All pretty near each other," Bannister said. "About ten miles from here."

"Show me," Fargo said and Bannister hurried off to get his horse. He returned on a brown mare and Fargo followed him across the edge of the prairie until he halted at a spot that bordered the bottom tip of the mountains. Fargo took in the wagons as he dismounted, their wheels smashed. His eyes searched the ground.

"They decided to wreck my wagons instead of driving them away. Just orneriness, I guess," Bannister said.

"They were being smart, not ornery," Fargo said. "They transferred the ore to other wagons in smaller amounts. That way they didn't leave any specially deep tracks."

"Which you came to look for," Bannister offered.

"That's right," Fargo said. "Now I'll be looking for other things."

"When do I hear from you?"

"When I've something to tell you," Fargo answered, taking to the saddle again as Frank Bannister rode off with a wave. Fargo moved on at a walk, his eyes sweeping the ground. The hijackers had not only transferred the ore in smaller amounts, they had covered their tracks. Fargo's experienced eyes picked up the signs of soil brushed over wagon tracks, and managed to follow the tenuous trail until it finally disappeared. He frowned as he stared at the edge of the mountains, aware the hijackers could have gone up into the low range. But they could have stayed clever and taken the prairie. Cursing softly, he chose the prairie. "They can't keep brushing over their tracks. It'd slow them down too much," he muttered aloud to himself.

He rode, pursued wheel marks that turned out to be false leads, and halted as night fell. He stayed awake after he ate, listening to the night sounds, with the hope that he could catch the creak of a wagon wheel, but he heard only the sounds of black-tailed prairie dogs, pocket gophers, and the distant howl of the red wolf. Finally, he slept and rose with the new day to take to the saddle again. But the day brought no leads and he took to searching the edge of the prairie. That brought him nothing more and after two days he decided to see if loose tongues might bring more than aimless searching. Turning, he headed the pinto back toward Almeda, aware that the Carter ranch was on his way. The ranch appeared as the day slid into late afternoon, larger than he'd expected, and he took in long corrals stocked with Herefords. The main house rose, a stone building with a slate roof, sturdy and impressive yet not pretentious.

As he drew up in front of the house, Amanda came from the rear, halting as she saw him, her eyes widening in surprise. Though dressed in work clothes, a denim skirt, and an old cotton shirt that hung loose and obscured the long line of her breasts, she still wore her hair up and somehow managed to look coolly patrician. "Fargo," she said. "Come to take my offer, I hope?"

"Sorry, just passing by. Stopped to see how you were doing," he said.

"We'll be driving a new herd soon," Amanda said and he found himself astonished at how regally lovely she looked. "I take it you're working for Frank Bannister," Amanda said.

"Right, but in a way I'm working for you, too," Fargo answered and Amanda frowned. "The varmints that attacked your herd were looking for Bannister's hijacked silver, I'm convinced."

"In a cattle drive?" Amanda frowned.

"In anything, anywhere, anyplace. I find who has the silver, those raids on your drives will stop," Fargo said.

"It's preposterous, the whole idea of it," Amanda snapped.

"Nothing's preposterous with all that silver up for grabs," he said and turned as he heard the front door of the house open. Angela emerged and halted when she saw him. Surprise and something more flooded her face, almost anger, he frowned inwardly.

"Fargo! What are you doing here?" Angela bit out.

"Now, that doesn't sound as though you're glad to see me," he commented.

She rushed forward, threw her arms around him, pressed the high, round breasts into his chest. "I'm sorry. Is that better?" she said, planting a kiss on his lips.

"Much," he said. Amanda's face tightened.

"It's just that I didn't expect to see you. I guess it was shock," Angela said, linking her arm in his. "Come inside," she said, and pulled him along with her into the house, where he found himself in a large, well-furnished living room with a deep leather sofa and thick rugs on the floor. She led him to the sofa, pulling him down beside her. "You didn't answer me. What brings you here? You finished your job for Frank Bannister already?"

"No. I'm on my way to Almeda," Fargo said.

"What do you hope to find there?" Angela questioned.

"Not find. Listen. Pick up stray talk. Nobody works in a vacuum, not hijackers or silver smugglers," Fargo said.

Her arms slid around his neck and her lips found his again, the kiss longer, wetter this time. "I'd ask you to stay but I couldn't relax under Amanda's nose.

Besides, I've set myself to wait for the right time and place, when this is over," she said.

"I've had plenty practice waiting," Fargo said. Her arms were still around his neck when Amanda entered.

"Sorry," Amanda said, the single word made of ice.

Angela pulled her arms down. "Just saying good-bye. He can't stay, not even for dinner," Angela said and stepped back.

"I'll come back when I get a chance," Fargo said and walked to the door. He was outside when he saw Amanda following. She halted beside the Ovaro with him.

"It seems Angela has taken quite a liking to you," she said, her words carefully measured.

"She's impulsive. Your words," he returned.

"And vulnerable," Amanda said. "People such as Angela are too quick to reach out. They're usually sorry afterward."

"Some people are too slow. They're sorry, too, maybe sorrier," he said evenly and saw the pink slowly suffuse her face.

"I've promises to keep," she murmured after a moment. "I told you that."

"So you did," he said as he pulled himself onto the horse. She kept her face carefully composed, he saw. "Good luck on your drive," he said, and as he spurred the Ovaro forward, he was aware of her eyes following him until he was out of sight. He headed for Almeda, reached it after night fell, and dismounted in front of the saloon. He entered Tequila Noches and the memories came back again. Little had changed inside the place, even to where the madam stood in a corner that gave her a sweeping view of the swinging doors.

He strolled toward her and took note of the figures gambling at a dozen tables. Most were playing poker, a few blackjack and twenty-one, still fewer whist. He smiled inwardly as he found Clyde Keyser standing at the door to his inner office, still sporting a flowered vest and a fancy, ruffled shirt, the small, ivory-gripped, short-barreled Beaumont-Adams pistol in his belt, a five-shot, accurate, double-action weapon. Fargo halted at a small table beside a larger one where five men were concentrated on their poker game with three others looking on. He sat down and found the madam at his side in moments.

"Hello, big man. You've been here before," she said. "I never forget a face."

"Hello, Juanita. I never forget a name. Or other things," he said, glancing at the voluminous breasts that pushed up from the low-cut, shiny red gown. Her broad face crinkled with appreciation.

"That's nice to hear," she said. "That what brought you back?"

"Sorry. Just passing through, looking to buy the right information," he said. "But first a bourbon and a beef sandwich."

Juanita waved at a younger woman in an abbreviated maid's outfit, pretty enough in a brassy way, and gave her Fargo's order. "What kind of information?" she asked Fargo when the girl left.

"Information, loose talk, even rumor," he said. "About hijacked silver."

"Hell, I'll sell you all you want of that." Juanita laughed, the large breasts jiggling. "Won't be worth anything, though."

"Try me. I'll decide on what it's worth," Fargo said and she lowered herself into the chair across from him and told him a parade of rumor and talk about the silver. Her evaluation had been right, he decided. None of it held anything useful, a lot of it purely wild speculation. "Maybe your boss knows something better," Fargo muttered.

"Doubt it," the woman said. "If he did he'd be telling his little favorite."

"Who's that?" Fargo inquired.

"One of the Carter sisters," the madam said and Fargo knew surprise swept through his face. The woman's sharpness caught it at once. "You know them?" she questioned.

"Met them. Which one is it?" Fargo asked.

"Angela, of course. Amanda's a pain in the ass to Clyde, always hovering about. He'd like to find a way to get rid of her but Angela depends on her. She's the one who runs the ranch."

"So it seems," Fargo agreed. "How much of a favorite is she to Keyser?"

"Don't really know but it seems to me that he's doing most of the panting," the madam said and Fargo found himself wondering if Amanda might have good reason to rein in Angela's impulsiveness. The waitress interrupted his thoughts as she brought his bourbon and a thick beef sandwich. The madam moved away and Fargo began his dinner as his attention was pulled to the table next to him. One of the players exploded in exasperation.

"Goddamn, lost again," the man swore and Fargo took in a slender, well-dressed figure, middle-aged with graying hair, a face some would call sensitive. Fargo found it weak.

"Your deal, Doc," one of the other players called out, a beefy man with a handlebar mustache and worn cowhand clothes. A thick shock of black hair fell over a low forehead. Next to him, a bald-headed man with small eyes sat. The other players were ordinary in appearance, one a smallish man with nervous hands.

"Seven-card stud," the man they'd called Doc called out, adjusting his brown coat jacket as he began to deal. Fargo sipped his bourbon as once again Doc lost. Ostensibly paying attention to his meal, Fargo watched with quick, unobtrusive glances, his attention drawn toward two men who looked on from behind the man called Doc. One, tall and thin with a sharp face, puffed on a cigarette. Beside him, a short figure with equally sharp eyes casually turned a pocket watch in his hands as he observed the game. When Doc lost for the fifth straight hand, Fargo's eyes had narrowed and he watched as Doc waved over Clyde Keyser.

The gambler approached, halting at Doc's elbow. "Got to buy more chips, Clyde. Rotten run of luck," Doc said.

"It happens," Keyser said, taking a wad of bills from his pocket and peeling off five to Doc. "That makes a thousand, counting last night," he said.

"You keep score, Clyde," the man said as Keyser sauntered away. Fargo kept the frown of surprise from his face but his inner signals were vibrating. Something was very wrong. Perhaps more than one thing. The man bought more chips and plunged into playing again as Fargo watched him promptly lose the next two hands. Fargo's quick glances moved across the two men looking on and he felt the anger rising inside him. As Doc entered the next hand, Fargo saw the other players grow cautious, particularly the beefy-faced one and the small-eyed bald one. After a few rounds of bets, both turned down their cards and dropped out. Another man called and stayed in and Doc spread his cards on the table, an ace-high full house. "Dammit, a real good hand at last and you boys fold and I don't win any real pot," Doc said in disgust.

But Fargo had seen more than enough. "That's because you're being taken, mister. They knew you had a hand they couldn't beat," he said and Doc turned to stare at him as did the others. Fargo sat quietly, well aware of the dangers of flinging an accusation down in a poker game, but he had a built-in hate for card cheats. "Those two are playing partners. They've been cheating you on every hand. The two gents behind you are iteming," Fargo said, using the term known to every gambler and card shark. It described a signaling process, sometimes the flick of an eyebrow, sometimes touching the nose, often puffing cigarette smoke, and sometimes swinging a pocket watch left meant bet, swinging it right meant fold.

"That kind of talk will get you real dead real fast, mister," the beefy one snarled.

"Goddamn right," the bald one echoed.

Fargo saw Doc staring at him, a frown digging into his forehead. "You sure about this, mister?" the man asked.

"Damn sure," Fargo said.

The beefy one's voice rose in a roar. "Son of a bitch," he spit out. Fargo saw his right hand move toward his gun. But Fargo's hand already rested on the butt of the Colt at his side, his sequence of targets already chosen. The two standing would be first. The two at the table would be a fraction slower in getting their guns out. Fargo snapped the Colt into his hand, fired, all in one, smooth, lightning motion. The two men standing behind Doc flew backward, both doubling over simultaneously as two shots slammed into their abdomens. The beefy one had his gun up and out but Fargo's third shot hurtled into his chest before he could fire. He flew backward, overturning his chair as he did. The bald-headed one lost a precious split second glancing at his partner. He tried to bring his six-gun around and realized he was too late. Fear flooding his face, he let the gun drop from his fingers as he screamed, "No, no, Jesus no," he cried.

Fargo brought the Colt around in a sweeping arc, crashed it into the man's temple, and the figure toppled sideways from his chair. Fargo stepped forward, kicked the man's gun away, and holstered his own Colt. "You've a sheriff here, I'd guess," he said to Doc. "He can lock that one up. Call the buryin' man for the others."

"My God, I've been losing to them for two days. No wonder," Doc said, taking his eyes from the still figures on the floor. "I owe you, mister, real big. Who are you?"

"Fargo . . . Skye Fargo."

"I'm Elroy Carter," the man said.

"Carter? Seems a popular name in these parts," Fargo said.

"That tells me you've met Angela and Amanda," the man said.

"I have. Related to you?"

"My nieces," Carter said, turning as Clyde Keyser came up. "Dammit, Clyde, what kind of people you letting in here these days?" he said accusingly.

The saloon owner offered a calm half smile. "Come on, Doc. I can't check the history of everybody who comes in. You've got to be careful when you play with strangers, stay alert, watch everything," he said, turning a full smile on Fargo. "Like this here gent did. That was damn fancy shooting, mister."

"His name's Fargo," Doc Carter said.

"I expected they'd do just what they did. I was ready for them," Fargo said.

"You sure were," Clyde Keyser said.

"I've had enough cards for tonight," Doc Carter cut in. "I'll have a few drinks and turn in. We'll settle up tomorrow, Clyde."

"Of course," Keyser said pleasantly.

"Maybe I can find a way to repay you sometime," Doc Carter said to Fargo. "You see Angela and Amanda you tell them what you did for me."

"I will." Fargo nodded and the man hurried away, planting himself at the bar.

"The meal's on the house, Fargo," Clyde Keyser said. "You did everybody a favor."

"I've seen too many men ruined by card sharks," Fargo said as the floor was cleaned. "I'm surprised you didn't catch what was going on," he added blandly.

"Can't see everything everywhere. I have to keep an eye on the whole room," Keyser said.

"Suppose so." Fargo smiled.

"What brings you to these parts, Fargo?" the saloon operator asked.

"Frank Bannister called me in," Fargo said.

Keyser's brows lifted. "Guess I know what for," he said, amusement in his voice.

Fargo let his half shrug answer. "I'd be obliged to know if you've heard anything," he said.

"I think you're on a wild-goose chase, Fargo. I think Bannister's hijacked silver is long gone," Keyser said. "You're wasting your time trying to chase it down."

"But only a small part of it has shown up in Dodge and Wichita," Fargo said.

"That's all Bannister's heard about. I say the rest of it's there. He just doesn't know it," Keyser said and Fargo's lips pursed. It was a possibility he hadn't contemplated. Nor had Frank Bannister, obviously. "There's not a wagon crossed the prairie that hasn't been searched by Bannister's people or others. The silver's already gone, I tell you. It's a waste of time to keep searching," Keyser said.

"Maybe," Fargo allowed.

"Another bourbon here," Keyser said to the waitress and strolled away with a friendly smile. Fargo sat back and watched Keyser move through the saloon with smooth affableness as the room returned to business as usual. But something was wrong. Something didn't fit, Fargo murmured to himself as he sipped his drink. He saw Doc Carter at the bar, drink in hand, and Clyde Keyser seemed unbothered by anything that had happened. But Clyde Keyser was too experienced a gambling man not to have seen that Doc Carter was being cheated. Why did he keep lending him more money? It was out of character for a man such as Keyser. It was as if he was perfectly willing to see Carter lose and go into his debt. Fargo mused a little longer and then turned off his thoughts. He needed more to come up with the answer, he realized. Perhaps Angela or Amanda could help. He tabled the thought, finished his bourbon, and sauntered from the saloon. The questions would stay, he knew, and he went outside into the dark of the night and pulled himself onto the Ovaro.

The town was dark and silent and he let the horse slowly walk down the wide single street through the center of town, the stores and warehouses on both sides locked and shuttered. He was nearing the last of the sheds and storage buildings that marked the end of town, the only sound the soft clip-clop of the pinto's hooves. The silence and the night warmth were enough to dull the senses and they would have, to most men. But the Trailsman wasn't most men. Like the wild creatures he had come to know and live with so often, he had learned to hear with their special hearing, always alert to the tiniest differences in the faintest of sounds.

He was at the end of town when the soft tattoo of the Ovaro was joined by another sound, intrusive, improper. He caught it at once, the faint scrape of a boot against wood. His reaction was instinctive and instant. He dived sideways from the saddle, hitting the ground just as the shots rang out. He counted four as the horse bolted. Rolling, Fargo flung himself into the deeper black shadows along the front of a warehouse and the Colt was in his hand as he came up on one knee, staying against the building wall. He heard movement across the street, footsteps on the wood entrance to the shed opposite from where he waited. Three men at least, he counted, perhaps five. Staying motionless, not drawing a breath, Fargo waited, letting his ears guide his eyes as he peered into the darkness. Suddenly the boards creaked again, to the right of the shed, and he saw the two figures, running in a crouch, starting to dart across the street toward his side. A volley of covering fire erupted from in front of the shed as the men ran. But it was wild, unfocused, and he heard bullets thudding into the building on all sides of him.

Fargo waited, letting the two figures reach the middle of the street before he fired, two shots so close together, they sounded almost as one. Both figures seemed to go into a strange, jerky dance before they pitched to the ground, one half atop the other. Fargo rolled, managing to get out of target range as another volley of covering fire erupted, this time smashing into the spot where he had been. Lying prone on the ground at a corner of the shed, he caught a glimpse of a third figure trying to race across the street. The Colt barked again and Fargo heard the man's half scream as he fell, groaned again, and lay still. Fargo peered through the night, his finger on the trigger of the Colt, when he heard the sound of footsteps racing along the back of the building through the pitch black shadows.

He waited, the Colt raised to fire. But seconds later he heard hoofbeats, two horses going into a full gallop. He rose and ran forward, but the hoofbeats were already growing faint. They'd be past hearing by the time he got the Ovaro and gave chase. He muttered a curse, halted, and holstered the Colt. He hadn't expected the card sharks to have friends waiting but they plainly had. They had learned of what had happened inside the saloon and waited to take revenge. Fargo whistled softly, the Ovaro appeared, and he climbed into the saddle. Riding slowly, he saw where the two men had fled from behind the last of the buildings, and he took note of a road that led between a double row of cottonwoods.

It was too dark to pick up a trail, he realized, deciding to return in daylight. If there was a trail to find, he'd find it, he was certain. Turning west, he rode until he found a spot under a cluster of hackberry, unsaddled the horse, and set out his bedroll. He went to sleep with questions hanging in his mind. Not about card sharks and their friends. They were understandable, their actions entirely in keeping with what they were. It was Clyde Keyser whose actions didn't fit what he was. Fargo's mouth was a tight line. Things that didn't fit always bothered him, even when he slept.

4

Fargo found himself riding west when morning came, Clyde Keyser still in his thoughts and vengeful card sharks almost unimportant. He reached the Carter ranch to find Amanda dragging a heavy sack of cattle feed to a shed. He dismounted and helped her take the sack into the shed. "Thanks. All the hands are busy in the corrals. Angela's with them," Amanda said. Something flat, almost grim, in her voice, made him study her even, patrician features.

"Trouble?" he asked, glancing at the way her longish breasts swayed under a light cotton shirt, again admiring how regal she could appear while doing very unregal chores.

"Just a disagreement. We have them," she said.

"You and Angela?" he inquired and she nodded. "Thought you were pretty much in charge of the ranch," he remarked.

"I am but it's not that simple," Amanda said. He heard the dismissal in her voice and didn't press her further. "What brings you back? Couldn't stay away from Angela?" she tossed out.

"Ouch. Got your claws out this morning, I see," he said.

"It happens," she said, no apology in her voice, and

he studied her again. Perhaps Angela wasn't the only complex one, he mused. His thoughts broke off as Angela appeared, saw him, and rushed over. Wearing a loose sweater and torn jeans, she was still curvy and sensual, he noted as her arms came around him, her lips finding his.

"Another surprise visit?" she said when she pulled back.

"Sort of. Had a surprise of my own. Met Doc Carter," Fargo said.

"Uncle Elroy? When and where?" Angela asked.

"Last night, at the Tequila Noches," Fargo told her.

"Figures," Amanda snapped coldly and he saw Angela's eyes narrow at her.

"Why is he called Doc?" Fargo questioned.

"Because that's what he is, a doctor," Angela said.

"A doctor with problems, gambling and drinking," Amanda cut in. "A doctor nobody goes to unless they have to. He's been reduced to treating animals and gunshot victims."

"Amanda doesn't like our uncle," Angela said.

"I don't like weak people who waste their lives," Amanda returned.

Fargo held Angela with his eyes. "Is she right about him?" he queried.

"He's a brilliant surgeon. He can make an incision clean as a whistle," Angela said.

"When his hand's steady enough and his mind can concentrate on something besides poker chips," Amanda put in.

"He'll get over his problems," Angela said. Amanda made a derisive sound as she walked away to disappear inside the shed. "She doesn't care about people," Angela said.

"She cares about you," Fargo said.

"Because of Pa," Angela said and Fargo heard the ice in her voice, and found himself wondering if it was ingratitude or perceptiveness. He decided to voice the thought that came into his mind.

"Clyde Keyser seems to care about Doc," he said. "He bankrolls him when he's losing big money. I'm wondering if that's because of you."

"Me?"

"Helping Doc would make him look good with you. Word is you're his favorite," Fargo explored.

"Gossip," Angela said. "He's invested in some steers we bought."

"He's not sweet on you?"

A coyness touched her face. "He likes me. I'd think you could understand that," she said and her lips came to his, clinging until she pulled away.

"I sure can," he admitted and her smile was quiet triumph. "I've got to get back to the corral. The hands are waiting for me to tell them which steers we'll be driving. Will you be back before we go on the drive?"

"Don't know," he said.

"Try," Angela said and hurried away. He took the reins and led the Ovaro behind him. He crossed the ground to pause at the shed and Amanda came outside.

"Leaving?" she asked and he nodded. "You came with questions. You get the answers?" she asked.

"Some," he said. "We talked about Doc and how Clyde Keyser's real friendly with him."

"Can't get a handle on that." Amanda frowned. "But it's true."

"It's fine with Angela," Fargo said.

"I told you, Angela's too quick to accept people,"

65

Amanda said. "And you've no need to repeat what you said. I've a good memory," she snapped.

"Wasn't going to." He laughed.

"But you were thinking it," she said. Her eyes held on him. "Angela tell you what we've been arguing about all morning?"

"No. Why don't you tell me?" he said.

She thought for a moment. "Doc figured into it," she said.

"Go on."

"No. She didn't tell you. I won't," Amanda said. He smiled. Anger and loyalty, ambivalence churning through her.

"Good luck on your drive," he said.

"You notice I didn't ask you to join us this time," she said.

"Figured you'd just stopped trying," he said.

"Decided it'd be too hard to trust you with Angela on a long drive," Amanda said.

"That's unkind," he said.

"But true," she returned. "The way she acts with you, comes on to you, I'd say you've already had your way with her if I didn't know better."

"But you know better," he said.

"Of course. You haven't had the chance. That's why I don't want you on the drive," Amanda said. "I'm not one to push fate."

"What do you call guarding Angela the way you do?" he asked.

"Keeping promises," Amanda said after a moment. Then she turned and went into the shed. He climbed onto the Ovaro and rode away. Sisters most always had complex relationships. These two were perhaps more complex than most, he reflected as he rode.

Amanda's answers about having promises to keep didn't tell the whole of it. Nor did Angela's accusations of her sister's coldness. There was a lot unsaid on both sides, he decided as he put the pinto into a fast trot.

When he returned to the outskirts of Almeda he rode into the twin rows of cottonwoods, slowing as he scanned the ground. There were some fresh hoofprints but not too many and he quickly found those he sought, the prints of two horses riding together and fast, their hoof marks dug deep into the soil by their gallop. He followed, turning out of the cottonwoods as the trail led west, then north into the foothills of the Sangria range. They had stopped to rest and he noted the marks where they had stretched out on the ground. They'd gone on, the trail showed, probably when morning came, and once again he followed. The trail led from the foothills into the mountains and he felt the furrow cross his brow. He slowed, and as he studied the prints the furrow dug deeper into his forehead. The tracks showed no hesitation, no wandering, no pauses to decide which way to go. The two men knew just where they were going and as he followed through mountain passes, the furrow on his brow became a deep frown.

For a pair of dry-gulchers on the run, the men had gone a long way, Fargo thought to himself, too long a way. They could've found many a spot to hide out long before this. The thought still pushed at him when the passage opened onto the mouth of a cave. He halted, backed the horse up, the Colt in his hand. Listening, he heard no sound and he swung from the saddle, moving carefully forward on foot. The mountain footing was mostly stone, thinly covered with soil, and trickier to read. But outside the cave, he picked up the prints of half a dozen horses besides the two he'd been trailing. Keeping his ears strained, he moved forward, but there was only silence as he edged his way into the cave. Reaching a deep and high-roofed opening, he halted. There was none of the usual cave smell, dank, damp, with the odor of stale bear and badger urine.

Instead, his nostrils were assailed by a sharp, acrid odor he didn't recognize, all of it coming from two large metal kegs open at the top and standing against the cave walls. He strode to the kegs and peered in. They were empty, but the odor grew stronger as he neared them. They were unmarked, he noted, and he saw a shovel and a pair of wooden chutes, not unlike the riffle boxes called Long Toms that were used to separate gold in gravel. He scanned the cave again and strode outside to where a trail of hoofprints led away from the other side of the cave and down a wide passage lined with high granite formations. He followed on the Ovaro, keeping sight of the thin layer of prints until the passage ended at the mouth of another cave.

The horses had halted where they stayed grouped together outside the cave entrance. A trail of footprints went back and forth from the cave. Fargo dismounted again, went into the cave, and found two more metal kegs and the same sharp, acrid odor. This time he saw something that resembled a large wooden hopper against one wall of the cave. He went outside, took to the saddle, and followed the trail where the riders had gone on west down mountain paths. But suddenly he reined up, swearing softly. He'd lost them on terrain that had turned to hard stone with not a tree or a bush to show a trail, not even loose pebbles to read. They were gone and that included the two fleeing dry-gulchers.

Only now Fargo found himself turning a new question in his mind. Had the dry-gulchers ever been friends of the card sharks in the saloon? Suddenly it was becoming less than likely. Suddenly their long flight into the mountains took on new dimensions. There was no reason for a pair of fleeing card sharks to go directly to the two caves. Damn, he swore. The dry-gulchers had never been friends of the card sharks in the saloon. He'd made the wrong assumption, he realized, a natural but wrong guess. Now, a very different picture began to come together. Word had gotten around that Bannister had hired him. There'd been more than enough time for that. News traveled quickly, gossip a pastime in this remote country. The dry-gulchers had their own reasons to try to kill him, none of them to do with card sharks and revenge.

He turned the Ovaro and began to retrace his steps, his jaw a hard line. He finally came out of the mountains and rode east till he reached Frank Bannister's place. The man came from the house to meet him, a mixture of surprise and hope in his face. "Get your horse," Fargo said.

"You find something?" Bannister asked.

"Yes, but I'm not sure what. I need you to use your nose," Fargo said and Bannister frowned. Hurrying away, he soon returned on his brown mare. Fargo led the way back into the mountains to where he had found the first of the caves. He dismounted and went inside, Bannister at his heels. He watched Bannister halt, draw in a deep breath, and frown at the two metal kegs. "Mean anything to you?" Fargo queried.

"By God. Sodium cyanide," Bannister said. "That's what you're smelling. They're using the new chemical refining method from Scotland."

"Fill me in," Fargo said.

"It's called cyanidation and it was designed to use on silver and gold imbedded deep in ore. They found the silver and gold could be loosened and dissolved in a weak solution of sodium cyanide, then recovered by running the metal through zinc shavings. These bastards have found that cyanidation can loosen silver enough to break into small pieces," Bannister said.

"Which they can smuggle through easier," Fargo said and Bannister nodded grimly.

"It's a variation of the original use of cyanidation. The beautiful thing about it is that all it takes is the sodium cyanide, zinc flakes, a few shovels, and a separating box, no huge pounders, no big smeltering operations."

"They've been moving from one cave to another to play it safe," Fargo said.

"We know how they're extracting the silver now but that doesn't really help us. How are they getting it through? They've two hundred thousand dollars of my silver extracted into small pieces that they're getting to Dodge and Wichita. That hasn't changed a damn bit," Bannister said.

Fargo wanted to resent the man's angry words and realized he couldn't. Bannister was all too right. What had been discovered was almost academic, nice to know but the real question stayed. He climbed onto the Ovaro and rode from the cave, Frank Bannister beside him until the man finally slowed and turned his horse east. "I'll be at my place as usual. Stay in touch," Bannister said and Fargo, returning a nod, put the pinto into a trot and held a steady pace. He had already decided to return to Almeda. Right now, it was his only connection point. He'd been attacked there. Perhaps he'd be targeted again. It was what he welcomed in a perverse way, another chance to get some answers. It wouldn't be the first time he'd made a target of himself. One more time wouldn't matter, now that he was alert to the possibility. Perhaps Almeda harbored what he needed to find. Or perhaps it was only a grubby little town that held no more promise.

He'd find out, he told himself as the day began to slide to an end. Darkness had fallen when he reached Almeda and sauntered into the saloon. He took a table once again alongside where Doc Carter was playing poker, this time with four new gambling partners. Carter saw him sit down and called out at once. "Welcome back, friend," he said. Fargo returned a smile as Clyde Keyser strolled over.

"Come to look out for Doc again?" the man asked. "I'm sure he'll be grateful for that."

"Came to eat," Fargo said evenly. "Looking for silver hijackers can make a man hungry," he added in a voice loud enough for most of the room to hear. He sat back, ordered a meal and a bourbon, and casually surveyed the room. His glances at Doc Carter and the others at the table told him the man wasn't being cheated. He was just not a very good poker player, betting too much on weak hands and too little on good ones and mostly not reading the cards well. Twice, he had to call on Clyde Keyser for more chips, Fargo noted, and once again Keyser supplied the money without hesitation. It still didn't fit. Even if Keyser wanted to curry favor with Angela, it didn't fit. Every man carried the patterns of his past, his life, especially men such as Clyde Keyser. He was a real gambling man and such a man wouldn't lay out the amount of cash he was bankrolling for a woman's favor.

Pussy, no matter how enticing, was like a weak poker hand to men such as Clyde Keyser, never a sure thing and never worth more than a few raises. That philosophy was ingrained, too much a part of the man to change. Yet he continued to bankroll Doc Carter. There had to be another reason, Fargo thought as he set the question aside. It didn't help in finding silver hijackers. Yet it would continue to intrigue him, he admitted as he finished his meal, sipped another bourbon, and finally strolled from the saloon. Once again, he walked the Ovaro through the town, a dark, silent place, but this time his ears were tuned to the slightest sound, his eyes sweeping the shadows for a hint of motion. But nothing materialized and finally he rode on across the open land to bed down under the same cluster of hackberry he had the night before.

When morning came, he breakfasted on a stand of prickly pear, the fruit of the cactus settlers often called Indian figs, using his slender throwing knife to slit the skin and scoop out the pulp. He found a trickle of water and finally rode into the flatland, close to the edge of the low rocks that began the mountains. He let the horse walk, scanned the rocks to his left, and squinted into the distance, and felt the furrow touch his brow. The furrow stayed as the horse and rider appeared ahead of him. As it took on shape and form, he saw long brown hair pulled high on her head, a white cotton shirt beneath which breasts swayed gently. "Amanda. What are you doing out here?" he asked as she halted before him.

"We'll be driving the herd in a few days. Thought I'd look for tracks, signs of trouble," she said.

"You'll find it riding alone out here," he said.

"I'm not with wagons, not even driving a single rig," she said.

"You think that's the only reason that could get you in trouble out here?" He frowned.

She gave an impatient shrug. "Seems like the going one these days," she said.

"Guess again," he said. "Don't turn your head but sneak a look across at that low line of rocks," he said, as he watched her glance with her head lowered. "You see a tiny gray spiral?" he asked and she nodded. "Trail dust. They've been watching you since before I came along."

"They're probably looking for wagons," she said.

"Probably, but they won't turn down a little extra fun that happens their way," he said and saw the alarm form in her eyes.

"We run for it?" she questioned.

"No. They'll have the advantage, likely put a bullet in me as they come after us. I need time to take them by surprise, even thirty seconds of time will do it, enough to get the drop on them."

"How?" Amanda asked.

"I'll be leaving you, riding off. You go on just as you've been," he said, seeing the uncertainty in her eyes. "It's our only chance. They'll come for you as soon as I'm gone. Run when they do, but they'll catch you. I want them concentrating on you. That'll give me the extra seconds I'll need."

"You don't even know how many there are," she said.

"The dust spiral's too thin for more than five or

73

six," he said. "You just go on as you were, not looking up at the rocks. They've got to think I'm gone or it won't work."

"All right," she said but she was distinctly unhappy, a frightened doe expression in her eyes. He backed the pinto, made a show of tipping his hat to her, and rode away, not glancing back. He stayed at a fast canter until he was sure he was a fading dot on the horizon, finally pulling the horse to a halt. Turning, he fought down the impulse to send the Ovaro into a gallop and kept the horse at a walk. If they followed what he thought they would, they'd be sweeping out of the rocks and onto the prairie by now. Amanda would be beginning to flee and he let the picture unfold in his mind as he continued to walk the Ovaro. He gave them another sixty seconds to catch her and pull her from her horse.

They'd surround her as they dismounted. They had no need to rush now. He let the Ovaro go into a trot, then sent the horse into a gallop. He was in sight of the still-tiny knot of figures. They'd hear him quickly enough but he'd be closer and he drew the big Henry from its saddlecase and had it up to his shoulder as the Ovaro thundered forward. The figures took on form— six men in a half circle, and dismounted, Amanda in the center of them. They were in his sights as they heard him and he saw them turn in surprise. But the powerful, long-range rifle was firing as he moved the weapon a fraction of an inch with each shot. Three of the men bucked as they went down and he glimpsed Amanda throwing herself to the ground. A fourth figure managed to get his gun up when Fargo's shot sent him almost somersaulting backward.

He swung the rifle at the fifth man, saw him dive,

land atop Amanda, yank her around, and put a six-gun to her head. The last, sixth figure got off two shots, too fast and too wide, but Fargo yanked the Ovaro to a halt and leaped to the ground, and staying almost flat as he landed, he aimed the rifle but held back firing as the man's voice snarled at him. "I'll blow her head off," he said and Fargo heard a Mexican accent. His glance went to the sixth man, who wore a flat-brimmed straw hat and stayed in a half crouch. Fear held his face tight. He had just witnessed the marksmanship that had all but wiped out the rest of his friends and he saw the rifle barrel pointed directly at him. "Get the horses," the man holding Amanda shouted.

"Move and you're dead," Fargo said. The man stayed frozen in place, uncertainty and fear in his small eyes.

"Get the horses," the other one shouted again. "He won't shoot. He knows I'll kill her."

Fargo flicked a glance at the one holding Amanda and saw desperation in his face. Fargo cursed silently. The man was a cornered rat, driven by self-preservation. He'd not hesitate to shoot. He was on the brink of panic. He, too, had seen the others taken down by impeccable marksmanship. Fargo's glance went back to the sixth man, who was starting to edge to the horses. His finger twitched on the trigger of the rifle but he knew he didn't dare shoot. The man brought two horses back to the one holding Amanda and Fargo shifted his aim. But the man cunningly put himself and his captive on the other side of the horses as he pulled Amanda to her feet. He kept her there as he hoisted her on the horse and had the gun to her temple again as he swung on behind her.

Again, Fargo swore silently. He couldn't risk a shot. Even if he hit his target, the man's finger might tighten on the trigger in a reflex action. He stayed prone as the two men raced away with Amanda, pushing to his feet as they vanished into the low rocks. Pulling himself onto the pinto, he jammed the Henry into its saddlecase, exchanged it for the Colt, and took off after the fleeing riders. He followed their path into the rocks, heard them take a side cut, then another, and stayed after them. They'd hear him following and he hung back, closing slowly and listening to the sound of their horses.

He turned a curve in the rock-lined passage when he yanked the pinto to a halt. Hoofbeats raced on ahead of him but a hard smile edged his lips. They were being clever and they'd have fooled most men. But they were dealing with someone whose ears were tuned to distinguishing the slightest variations in sound. Only one set of hoofbeats were racing on, clattering along the stone-walled passage. The other had halted, lying in wait for him to charge after the hoofbeats and into a hail of lead. Fargo slid from the Ovaro and ran forward on steps silent as a mountain lion sensing its prey. Staying against one wall of rock, he slowed as the passage grew wider and he saw the niche in the opposite wall. Dropping into a crouch, he crept another dozen feet and halted, his ears straining. He hadn't more than thirty seconds to wait for the sound echoing from inside the niche, the faint tinkle of a rein chain as the man tried to keep his horse quiet.

He was waiting, gun raised, for his target to charge into sight. But by now he was frowning, becoming aware that something was wrong. His target hadn't charged into view. Fargo stayed motionless. The man was no hunter, no tracker, no woodsman who knew the art of waiting. He was a small-time bandit without the inner discipline to wait. Fargo knew all he had to do was stay motionless until the man broke and charged from the niche. But the other one with Amanda was getting further away with every passing second. The sound of his hoofbeats was already growing faint. Fargo cursed inwardly. He couldn't play the waiting game. Amanda's life wouldn't permit it. Measuring the width of the niche, Fargo uttered another silent curse, gathered his powerful calf and thigh muscles, and flung himself forward, made a rolling ball of himself as he crossed in front of the opening in the rocks.

The man fired, but taken by surprise, he was split seconds late and his aim wild. Fargo heard the bullets slam into the rocks behind him as he somersaulted past the niche and came up on one knee. He was waiting as the man charged out of the niche to finish off his target. The Colt raised, Fargo stayed in place as the horseman raced into view. The man's eyes widened in surprise for the last time as Fargo's two shots hurtled into him. He fell backward from his horse, lifeless before he hit the ground.

Fargo rose, whistled, and the pinto trotted forward, skirting the still figure on the ground. Pulling himself onto the horse, Fargo started up the narrow rock passage, picking up the sound of the hoofbeats that were barely audible now. Following his ears, he turned down one passage into another, and the hoofbeats grew louder. But by now the man had heard the pinto. So far he probably assumed it was his friend racing to catch up with him. When he found out it wasn't, desperation would seize him again and desperation destroyed reason. Amanda's life would again hang on that very thin thread called panic.

Racing forward, Fargo searched for some way to prevent a standoff with the man and his hostage. He spied a small pass that led off to the right and quickly climbed higher into the rocks but paralleled the path he was on. He took it, keeping the Ovaro racing almost full-out, and caught sight of the man on the path below, Amanda in front of him in the saddle. He'd heard the other hoofbeats and Fargo saw him nervously glance backward and cast another glance seconds later. Fargo spurred the pinto on, passed the man below, and kept on, staying ahead of him as the passage began to turn downward.

Peering ahead, Fargo could see where the passage dipped again to come out joining the road below. He raced on, losing sight of the man below. He'd reach the spot where the roads joined in plenty of time to be waiting there when the man rode up. He'd have the advantage of surprise but, cursing softly, surprise wouldn't be enough. It wouldn't avoid the confrontation he wanted to prevent, that standoff with a desperation-filled rodent. He needed something more, the kind of surprise that would give him an advantage. His lips were pulled back as he reached the road below, his mind casting out with its own desperation when he spied the base of a broken paloverde against one side of the passage.

He pulled to a halt, had the lariat in his hand as he leaped from the horse. He ran to the stump of the tree and tied one end of the lariat around it. Laying the rope flat on the ground, he pulled it across the passage, then took the other end of the lariat and the pinto and went behind the rocks on the other side. Amanda could get a cracked rib or two, he realized, but a cracked rib was better than dead. Not more than a few moments passed when the man and Amanda appeared, his horse going full-out. Fargo saw the man frown as he cast another glance behind him. Eyes narrowed, Fargo focused on the horse's feet. When the mount's left forefoot went over the rope, he yanked the lariat up and pulled it taut with all his strength.

The horse pitched forward as he was tripped and Fargo saw the man and Amanda fly from the saddle. Both hit the ground simultaneously and he heard Amanda's half scream. He ran forward, the Colt in his hand. Amanda lay on the ground in a half daze as the man pushed to his feet and saw his gun on the ground some six inches from him. "Don't," Fargo said as the man started to reach for it. "Back off."

The man stopped, peered at him, and hesitated. He saw the Colt aimed at him but his eyes returned to the gun, so temptingly close. Then, as Fargo had seen done so often before, with that strange combination of bad judgment, bravado, and fear, the man's arm shot out for the gun. Fargo fired, and the man screamed in pain as the bullet shattered his wrist. Fargo stepped forward and kicked the gun away as the man clutched his wrist to his side, looking at him with defeat and resignation. "Go on, finish it. Kill me," he said.

"I could've done that just now," Fargo said and the man glowered back. Fargo shot a glance at Amanda. She was sitting up, rubbing her shoulder with one hand as she looked on wide-eyed. He brought his eyes back to the man. "What were you doing here?" he asked.

"We heard there was silver being smuggled," the man said.

"Figured that. Where are you from?" Fargo questioned.

"Sierra Blanca," the man said.

Fargo grunted. "Small-time *banditos*. You're not worth killing. Get your horse and ride."

"I can't use my wrist," the man said.

"You've got another one," Fargo said. "Ride before I change my mind."

The man looked at the ice-floe blue of the big man's eyes, swallowed hard, and pulled himself to his feet. Suddenly he realized he was very lucky. Too small-minded to be grateful, he pulled himself onto his horse and rode away, aware enough to know that looking back might be a mistake. Fargo stepped to Amanda and she came to him, arms reaching around his neck, her long-waisted form pressed against him. She held him tight but there was no trembling in her. "Thank you, oh, God, thank you," she murmured, continuing to cling to him until finally she pushed away, a hint of embarrassment in her face. "I'm sorry," she said.

"Why?" he asked mildly.

She straightened, composed her face into its usual containment. "I'm not Angela. I don't do things the way she does," she said, paused, and her hands came against his chest. "That doesn't mean I'm not grateful. I am, terribly. You must believe that," she said.

"I do," he said, the deep feelings in her brown eyes very honest and very real. "Let's go back and find your horse," he said, and leading her over to where the Ovaro waited, he pulled her into the saddle with him. She sat in front of him and as he reached around her to hold the reins he felt the soft sides of her breasts. When he walked the horse forward, she held her back stiffly, trying to sit as properly as possible with two in the saddle. "You ever relax?" he asked as they rode.

"It doesn't come easy to everybody," Amanda said and he turned the answer in his mind. It held a tinge of something, almost a wistfulness.

"It might if you let yourself try," he said.

"Angela relaxes enough for the both of us. It's always been that way," she said.

"Because you let it be like that," he said.

"It's what Pa expected of me. That's why he left things the way he did, divided up the way they are," Amanda said.

"How's that?"

"He left the ranch to Angela," Amanda said and Fargo's brows lifted.

"Thought you both owned the ranch," Fargo said. "What'd he leave you?"

"A yearly salary forever and the right to run the place," she said.

"Doesn't seem very fair dividing," Fargo said.

"He thought it was, given the other conditions he set," Amanda answered.

"Such as?"

"We have to share all income. He figured that way neither of us would have enough money to force the other out. Sometimes I think it was his way of ensuring I'd look after Angela."

"Seems to me like a recipe for resentment, a ranch neither of you really have," Fargo said. "I can see why Angela resents it and you."

"She's always resented being protected," Amanda said.

"How about you? Are you doing your own resenting in your own way?" he asked.

Amanda turned, looked at him, and smiled, a sudden gesture that filled her contained face with a flash of unexpected warmth. "That's a hidden question, Fargo," she said.

"How?"

"You're asking if my protecting her is really getting back at her," she returned.

He allowed a half smile at her acuity. "Is it?" he said.

She reflected a moment. "I like to think I do what's best for her. It's what I've always done."

"That could be more habit than caring," Fargo said.

"That's a cynical thing to say," Amanda tossed back.

"Maybe and then maybe it's the truth," he said as they came onto the plain and he nodded to his left. "There's your horse," he said and rode to the bay gelding. She slid from the saddle and climbed onto her mount and he came alongside her. He rode most of the way to the ranch with her as the day began to draw to a close. "You'll make it all right from here," he said. "No more lone exploring across the prairie."

"No," she said, reaching out and pressing his arm. "Thank you again, Fargo." He nodded and studied her for a moment. "What are you thinking?" she asked.

"You've told me a good deal. You want to tell me what you and Angela have been arguing about?" he said.

"No. It's her making. She can tell you if she likes," Amanda said.

"You've your own stubbornness, don't you?" he said.

"I call it principles," she said and put the horse into a trot. He turned and rode back west and it was night before he reached Almeda. The town still beckoned him. It was a place of strange undercurrents, of things that didn't fit. Perhaps it would still give up a clue, a lead.

5

He had just reached the edge of town when he knew something was different. His nose told him as it drew in the strong, almost pungent odor of cattle, a lot of cattle in one place. Next he saw the normally silent darkness was broken by a series of long torches in the ground on both sides of the main street. The street itself was filled with bellowing, restless, jostling steers, at least a hundred, he guessed. Cowhands on both sides of the herd kept the animals together. Fargo edged his way past the long line of cattle and the torches. There was a big barn lighted inside with kerosene lamps and at the far end, an empty corral. He took in the steers as he walked the pinto forward, seeing they were all Herefords. The furrow on his brow deepened as he drew closer to the barn. A dozen men carrying rifles ringed the structure. As he moved still closer, he saw a man carrying a burlap sack marked FEED enter the barn and come out moments later empty-handed.

Fargo sent the pinto toward the barn and one of the men stepped forward, swinging his rifle up. "That's far enough, mister," he said.

"Want to get to the other end of town," Fargo said, annoyance in his voice.

"Go around the back till you get there," the man said.

"Damn strange time and place to be herding cattle, isn't it?" Fargo said truculently.

The man shrugged. "Not my call. Just be on your way," he said. Fargo backed the pinto a few yards down the street and halted in the shadows of a darkened warehouse beside a narrow alleyway between the buildings. He let his eyes sweep the scene again. It was not only unexpected, it had a strange, almost unreal quality to it. Cattle weren't run through the center of town, not even by daylight, much less left waiting in the street. He'd wait, too, out of more than idle curiosity. He cast a glance at the mass of white-faced Herefords as questions piled on top of each other in his mind. He waited silently, watching the cowhands work to keep the herd quiet and in place, when the figure appeared on foot, striding toward the barn.

He stared as the figure took shape and became the tall, thin form of Doc Carter. The man walked briskly, carrying his little black doctor's bag in one hand. Another figure came into sight a few paces behind Doc and Fargo saw Clyde Keyser. As Doc Carter reached the door of the barn, Keyser motioned to the cowhands who cut two of the Herefords from the rest and drove them into the barn and closed the door behind them.

Fargo felt his curiosity spiraling but he stayed quietly in place. Clyde Keyser was leaning against the side of the building and lighting a cigar. The frown digging deep into his brow, Fargo guessed some fifteen minutes had passed when he heard the sounds from the rear of the barn. He backed the Ovaro down the black alleyway to the rear of the building and saw the rear door of the barn open and the two steers being let out into the adjoining corral. Fargo moved back through the alleyway to the main street in time to see the two cowhands emerge from the front of the barn, Doc Carter peering out in shirtsleeves. The hands cut another two steers from the herd and drove them into the barn and closed the front door again.

Fargo stayed, waited, and watched the pattern as it developed. Steers were brought into the barn in pairs, held there for some fifteen minutes, then let into the corral by the back door. Occasionally, Doc Carter stepped out for a moment, consulted with Keyser, and then returned to the barn. The rifle-bearing guards stayed in place at the corral and the barn. Finally, after the tenth pair of steers were brought into the barn, Fargo moved out of the deep shadows and walked toward Clyde Keyser. The man saw him approach, straightened up, and inclined his head in a wry smile. "Fargo. Thought you were out looking for hijacked silver," Keyser said. "And you show up here."

"Thought you were running a saloon and you show up with a cattle herd," Fargo returned. "You change jobs?"

"Protecting an investment," Keyser said.

"This is your herd?" Fargo frowned.

"I'm helping out the Carter girls. It's their herd," he said.

"Helping out how? What's Doc Carter doing here?"

"Vaccinating the steers," Keyser said.

"Against what?" Fargo frowned.

"Longhorn fever," Keyser said, his reference to the deadly fever that was decimating herds of longhorns all over Texas.

"First, it's something special to longhorns," Fargo said.

"There's been others, some Brahmins and some Herefords have gotten it," Keyser said.

"Second, nobody knows what causes it. Some folks think it might be due to a bug, a tick or maybe even an ant. Some say it's an airborne infection," Fargo said.

"The Doc thinks it comes with contact, a hide infection that rubs off, and he says he's got a vaccination against it," Keyser said. "On a long drive, you could run into longhorns. Angela didn't want to take any chances and liked the idea of a vaccination. As it is, we're only doing half the herd."

"Why only two at a time?"

"The Doc feels it's best that way," Keyser said.

"Why all the guards?" Fargo pressed.

"Had another herd a while back. Most of them were rustled out the minute they were vaccinated. I wasn't going to let that happen again."

"Why at night?"

"The Doc says the cattle are quieter then, easier to inject."

"What's your stake in this, Keyser?" Fargo asked.

"Vaccinating costs money. Angela said they didn't have the cash so I gave her a loan," the man said.

"You haven't mentioned Amanda in any of this," Fargo said.

"She didn't go along with Angela. She's been real unfriendly over it," Keyser said. "No matter, it's done."

"Seems so," Fargo said as another two steers were taken into the barn. "Guess I'll be moving on," he said, and turning the Ovaro, he rode from town. Clyde

Keyser's answers clung as he rode, irritating, bothersome, and he wrestled with his thoughts. Once again, things fitted yet really didn't fit. Clyde Keyser had offered reasonableness that skirted reason. Why two steers at a time, Fargo asked himself as he rode. Why not just go from one steer to another? A vaccination took only a needle jab, a matter of a few dozen seconds. Why at least fifteen minutes between each pair of steers? And why behind closed doors? Then there was Doc Carter. Were his services his payment for being bankrolled in his gambling losses? If so, why did Angela have to borrow from Keyser? It didn't fit properly, he thought as he rode from town to the cluster of hackberry where he bedded down. He'd questions to explore further, he decided as he drew sleep around himself.

When morning came, he woke, washed, and dressed and found another stand of prickly pear on which to breakfast before riding toward the Carter ranch. One more stray thought stuck in his mind. He certainly couldn't draw any connection between Clyde Keyser, Doc Carter, and hijacked silver but Keyser had tried hard to convince him that the silver was long gone in Dodge. Maybe a little too hard, Fargo pondered. Maybe Keyser knew more than he was saying. In any case, a little more nosing around might still turn up a lead. There was always the chance Keyser had let a remark slip to Angela. If not, he'd return to prowling the prairie, a prospect that didn't lend encouragement. He reached the ranch in midmorning, saw the corrals filled with the white-faced steers and a bunch overflowing outside under the watchful eyes of a cowhand.

Amanda, beside the barn with a pitchfork in hand,

saw him, put down the tool, and came over as he dismounted. Wisps of hay stuck in her hair, her face was shiny with a thin coat of perspiration, and her gray work shirt without cut or cling. Yet she somehow looked patrician, very much a part of her surroundings yet very much apart from them. Her long figure held itself regally, a dark blue skirt clinging to her long thighs. "Getting ready to start your drive?" he asked.

"Tomorrow morning, I hope. Some last-minute problems still to be worked out," Amanda said.

"Such as?"

"The hands are grumbling. I told them yesterday there'd be no chuck wagon and no supply wagon. I'm not asking for a repeat of last time. Every man will have his own rations to carry. They're grumbling because there'll be no chuck wagon hot meals," she said.

"You'll handle it, I'm sure," he said.

"I'll offer them a bonus," she said. "They'll come around. Extra cash is better than hot beans." Her eyes held his; they carried both warmth and reserve. She could mix opposites and carry it all off.

"Think I know what you and Angela have been arguing about," he said blandly and she waited. "Stopped in Almeda last night," he said. Her eyes narrowed and her patrician features became etched in ice. "Guess I'm right," he slid at her.

"That make you happy?" she snapped.

"Always like to be right," he said.

"It's ridiculous, all of it," Amanda said.

"The vaccinating?"

"That and borrowing from Clyde Keyser to pay for something that's a joke."

"What if it isn't a joke? What if Doc Carter has got hold of something?" he queried.

Amanda gave a derisive sniff. "You know nobody knows what causes longhorn fever. If they find out it'll be in some laboratory. Doc Carter's a surgeon, nothing more."

"He seems to think he's got something," Fargo said.

"Exactly. He thinks. I've got ideas, too. I bet it's some kind of bug, maybe a mosquito, maybe a kind of tick. All he wants to do is test out his crazy ideas on our cattle and that's not going to happen."

"Why not?"

"I see a herd of longhorns, I'll go thirty miles out of our way to stay away from them," she said.

"Angéla and Keyser went for his vaccinating," Fargo said.

"Clyde Keyser talked Angela into it. But that's Angela, too quick to listen to the wrong people, too susceptible, too easily swayed. That's why I try to keep her away from men like Clyde Keyser."

Fargo smiled at her. "You want to keep me from her. You said it'd be too hard to trust me on a long drive. I'd say that makes me one of those men."

She thought for a moment. "For different reasons," she said seriously.

"Such as?" he asked.

"I'm not going into that now," Amanda said.

"Better or worse reasons?" He laughed.

Her face stayed serious. "Different," she said again. She picked up her pitchfork as Angela came from the house, then turned and strode away. Angela let out a squeal of delight when she saw him and her arms were around his neck in moments, her lips warm and soft.

"Come to wish us luck?" she asked.

"Something like that," he said. Angela's arms stayed around his chest.

"How about you? Any luck on the silver hijackers?" she asked.

"Not yet," he said and his eyes went to the corral. "The steers from last night back in with the others?"

"Yes. You must've been in town," Angela said.

"I was, saw Doc Carter and Clyde Keyser," Fargo told her. "Your friend Keyser thinks the silver is all already in Dodge. He ever tell you why he's so sure of that?"

"No. Clyde's pretty tight-lipped. But if that's what he thinks I'd bet he's right. He'd have a reason for thinking that."

"He ever say he heard something?" Fargo pressed.

"Not to me," Angela said.

"People get confidential with someone they like," Fargo remarked. "And being in business together and all."

Angela's lower lips pushed out in a half pout. "Clyde's been very helpful."

"Amanda doesn't see it that way," he said.

"Amanda's afraid of everybody. She's afraid of herself," Angela snapped.

"That might be right," Fargo conceded. "But she's concerned with what's best for you. I believe that."

"I know what's best for me," Angela said, cutting off anything more by pressing her round, high breasts against his chest as her lips found his again. She finally pulled away but not before he'd felt the soft warmth of her twin mounds. "That's so you'll wait for me till I get back," she murmured.

"Count on it," he said.

"Now I've chores to do for tomorrow," she said, stepping back. "Hope you find the silver." He nodded, watching as she hurried past the corral, her rear bouncing with her every step. No cool containment for Angela, he thought as he climbed onto the Ovaro. He started to turn the horse when Amanda came from the barn, her eyes holding him, studying his chiseled face, saying nothing as she peered at him.

"Different reasons," she said finally, and turned and went into the barn.

He smiled as he rode from the ranch. Contrasts. One embraced sensuousness, the other rejected it, yet both could reach out, each in her own way. He rode slowly, returning to the edge of the mountains, skirting the places where paths led down to the prairie, his eyes sweeping the ground for prints. He found more than enough but they all wandered, riders searching, not smuggling. He halted when night fell, bedded down tired, and fought off discouragement. It was a condition that only fed on itself and when morning dawned hot and dry, he rode into the mountains. Finding a place that let him scan the prairie, he waited. The dust cloud came first, moving slow and wide, unmistakable, and then the herd came into sight in the distance.

At least two hundred steers, he guessed. They'd go east, straight across the upper part of Oklahoma Territory, and then swing north into Kansas and finally to Dodge. The trails to Dodge and Wichita were established, used by most cattle drives and wagon trains even though there were no markers across the plains. They'd not be hard to watch, for anyone, not Kiowa warriors and not those searching for silver being smuggled. He swept his eyes back and forth across the distant mass of cattle and a wry smile touched his face. No chuck wagon and no supply wagon. Amanda had had her way on that. He stayed, let the herd finally vanish over the horizon line, and threaded his way back down to the flatland. He thought about trailing the herd and decided against it. Without a single wagon, it was unlikely they'd target the herd and he rode south, finally turning west as he crossed and crisscrossed the plains.

He had searched into the midafternoon when, riding west, he picked out the line of wagons as they appeared. The frown on his brow grew deeper as he rode toward them. He counted five wagons, two of them Conestogas, three Owensboro Texas wagons with top bows on which to drape loose canvas. The wagon train slowed to a halt as he reached it and his eyes swept over some dozen occupants, families with three to four children, in what seemed a very typical train of settlers. But his eyes focused not on the families but on the four to six trunks the he could see in each wagon.

"'Afternoon, mister," the burly man driving the lead wagon called out, a heavy-set, pleasant-faced woman beside him. "Can we do anything for you?" he asked.

"Yes," he said. "Name's Fargo . . . Skye Fargo. You could answer me some questions."

"If we can. I'm Jed Bullock. This is my wife, Sarah," the man said.

"Where are you headed?" Fargo asked.

"Kansas. We'll follow the Cimarron to the Red Hills. Word has it there's good land for the taking there," Jed Bullock said.

"That'd be in the general direction of Dodge," Fargo said.

"Until we swing south," the man said.

"Where are you from?" Fargo queried.

"Utah. We took the long way around the Sangre range," the man said.

"Why are you asking, Fargo?" another man said, a wide-faced man with reddish hair. A petite woman and a little boy were seated beside him.

Fargo's eyes went to the trunks in each wagon before he answered. "Anyone tell you that wagon trains crossing this way are being attacked?" he asked.

"Kiowa? Cheyenne?" the red-haired man said.

"Neither. Men looking to take hijacked silver for themselves. It's general thought it's being shipped by wagon train," Fargo answered.

"No one said anything to us," Jed Bullock put in. "Fact is, we've been running into good luck."

"That's right," his wife added. "A businessman paid us a right nice price to take these trunks to Bucklin."

"What's in them?" Fargo questioned.

"No idea," Bullock said. "None of our business. He paid us. That's good enough."

Fargo glanced at the others, who nodded in agreement as they listened. He let his eyes pause on a half dozen youngsters in the third wagon. "I'd like to have a look in them," Fargo said.

"They're padlocked," Bullock said.

"And it wouldn't be right, us doing that," his wife put in. "He paid us, trusts us to get his property to him." Fargo swore silently. They were good, God-fearing people, not the kind to violate an obligation.

"What's your interest in all this, Fargo?" someone else called out.

"I've been hired to catch whoever's bringing the hijacked silver through," Fargo answered.

"You think it's in these trunks?" the redheaded man said.

"Don't know. That's why I'd like a look," Fargo said.

"That'd mean breaking open each one." The man frowned.

"No, we can't allow that," Sarah Bullock said. "He was a nice man, well-dressed, well-spoken. It just wouldn't be right."

"Where'd you meet him?" Fargo asked, hoping to ferret out a lead.

"In Almeda, when we laid over to get some repairs on the wagons," one of the men answered.

"He give you his name?" Fargo questioned.

"Clyde Keyser," the woman said. Fargo stared back for a moment as surprise swept over him and thoughts began to churn inside him, smashing into each other as they did. They were coming too fast. He needed time to sort them out.

"I think you folks ought to turn back, wait until things quiet down in these parts," he suggested.

"We can't do that. Time's important. We've got to set up living before winter comes," Bullock said.

"They're looking for wagon trains. They see you and those trunks and you can be damn sure they'll come attacking. You can't fight a band of gunhands with all the kids you have on hand," Fargo said.

"If we're attacked they can take the trunks. We won't fight over that," someone else said. "But you can't say for sure we'll be attacked, can you, mister?"

"I'm sure enough for me," Fargo said.

"That's not good enough for us," Bullock said.

"We appreciate your warning, Fargo, but it seems to us you're thinking more about silver than us," his wife said and Fargo grimaced inwardly at her accusation.

"We've given you enough time, Fargo. We'll be moving on," Jed Bullock said and snapped the reins over his team.

"Good luck to you," Fargo said and stayed as the wagons passed him and headed east across the prairie. Silently, he swore at decency. They were good, honest people with integrity, thrown into more than they knew. More than he knew, Fargo thought angrily. But they were on their way to being targets. They'd be spotted easily, prying eyes waiting for wagons as snakes wait for field mice.

Fargo stayed in place and began to sort out the thoughts that continued to churn through him. Was that silver in the trunks? If so, that'd damn clearly make Clyde Keyser the hijacker of Frank Bannister's silver. But if he headed the hijackers, why send the silver across the prairie in wagons. He had to know it was certain to be attacked. That didn't make any damn sense. Why had he paid those good families to take the trunks? The wagons would be a target, the sight of the trunks a red flag. A stroke of boldness? Arrogance? Fargo wondered. Did he think the wagons would be so obvious they'd be passed by? Or did he think they might just slip through?

Fargo spit in frustration. The explanation didn't hold water. Keyser was too smart to take that kind of gamble. Playing the odds was ingrained in him. Then why? What did it mean? The questions hammered at him but he knew one thing. Whatever the truth, he had sent five wagons full of innocent men, women, and children to an almost certain death. Knowing the ruthlessness of previous attacks, giving up the trunks wouldn't save the settlers. They'd not be left alive to talk or tell. Fargo swore again. He couldn't stand by and let that happen, wouldn't let families go to their deaths. Answers to questions could come later. He moved the Ovaro forward as the wagons grew small, almost out of sight. Riding just fast enough to keep them in his vision, he steered the Ovaro closer to the edge of the mountains where he could avoid being spotted on the open prairie.

The wagon train helped him without knowing it as they turned southeast to cut straight along the flatland. The last of the Sangre range was only a half mile away. From there, it'd be only open prairie and he found himself wishing for an attack while he still held an advantage. He'd ridden almost the half mile when he got his wish, turning the pinto into the last of the rocks as he saw the riders sweep down onto the prairie. He counted some dozen riders, gunhands who'd quickly be able to outshoot the five men in the wagons and the women who'd take up a rifle. Cutting behind a line of low rocks, he saw the wagon train pick up speed. They had spotted the horsemen racing at them and instantly recognized trouble.

Fargo spurred the pinto on, pulling the big Henry from its saddlecase as he saw the wagons pull to a halt, the attackers cutting them off and coming at them from both sides. Dropping from the saddle, Fargo ran along the line of rocks on foot, peering out at the wagons as he did. The shooting hadn't started. Jed Bullock would be trying to explain himself in order to avoid a shoot-out he'd be bound to lose. As Fargo watched, three of the horsemen dismounted, pulled two of the trunks from the first wagon, and threw them on the ground. As they started to toss out the other two, Fargo took aim and fired. Both men jerked in their tracks, dropped the trunks, and collapsed to the ground. The others spun, searching the land behind them. But Fargo had already raced another ten paces in a crouch, halted, and fired again. Another of the attackers pitched from his horse.

Racing to another spot, Fargo fired again and another figure toppled from his horse. The others recovered from their surprise and sent a volley of shots at the rocks, plainly unsure how many guns were firing at them. They spread out as they raced toward him and Fargo saw one of the riders drop from his horse as a round of shots erupted from the wagons. But the others ignored the shots from the wagons and kept racing toward the rocks, intent on taking care of the intruders. They knew they could always catch up to the wagons. Fargo aimed and fired, and another rider dropped from his horse but the others kept coming, spreading out further as they did. Fargo left the Ovaro out where they'd see the horse once they came into the rocks and clambered up onto a higher perch.

He was crouched low as the riders dropped from sight and reappeared again in moments inside the rocks, coming in from the sides. They reined to a halt as they saw the Ovaro and stared at the lone horse.

"What the hell?" one said. "Only one son of a bitch? I don't believe it?"

A flat-faced man with bushy black hair snarled his reply. "Find the bastard. He can't be far."

"He isn't," Fargo said as he fired from the high

rock. Two of the men instantly toppled from their horses, one to each side, almost like a grisly parody of a flower peeling away its leaves. The others looked up as Fargo's third shot caught the one with the bushy black hair. Hurtling from almost directly above him, the heavy rifle slug drove him into his saddle. He suddenly seemed half his size as he fell from his horse, his body compacted together. Fargo was bringing the rifle around when the last four turned, whipping their horses in a near gallop as they fled. He let another shot fly after them and heard one cry out in pain as they raced from the rocks. He waited as they reached the flatland below, staying at a gallop as they raced away, one bent low in the saddle and clutching his side. He watched as they rode on, happy to flee with their lives, and when they were out of sight he climbed down from the rock, swung onto the Ovaro, and rode out onto the plains.

The wagons were still in place, he saw, and Jed Bullock put down his rifle as he recognized Fargo. "By God, that was all just you?" the man said, awe in his voice.

"Nobody else," Fargo said.

"By God, that was some shooting. They thought a whole passel of guns was firing at them. So did we," Bullock said.

"They had us," the red-haired man said. "God knows what they would have done to us if you hadn't come along."

"Killed you, all of you. That's what they've been doing," Fargo said.

"We owe you, Fargo," Sarah Bullock said. "We should've listened to you in the first place."

"It's time for a look inside those trunks," Fargo

said. He brought the rifle up and blew the padlock from the nearest trunk on the ground. As the others gathered around, he opened the trunk, completely uncertain of what he'd find, all the contradictions still swirling through him. Pulling the lid up, he found himself staring at clothes carelessly thrown into the trunk, old clothes mixed in with bedsheets. He began pulling them out, came upon a blanket, then more clothes, and at the bottom, a half-dozen large rocks.

He stepped back, his lips a tight line, and blew the padlock from the second trunk. He rummaged through it, pulled out more old clothes, a pair of torn boots, and more rocks. "Take down all of them," he said and the rest of the trunks were deposited on the ground. He blasted each one open, emptied out each, and found they were all filled with the same old clothes and rocks to add weight. Jed Bullocks's voice cut into his thoughts. "Why'd anyone ship all this old stuff? All looks pretty useless to me," the man asked.

"It is. You've been used," Fargo said grimly.

"Why? For what?" Bullock asked.

"I don't know but I'm going to find out," Fargo said and heard the anger in his voice. "You folks go on your way now."

"You think we'll be all right from here?" Sarah Bullock asked.

"I'd expect so. It'll take a while for that bunch to get organized into another gang. But I'd leave the trunks right here. No sense drawing attention to yourselves," Fargo said.

Jed Bullock nodded, shook his hand, and climbed into his wagon and led the others away. Fargo watched them go, then spent a moment more staring at the trunks scattered on the ground. They seemed to rise up at him, filling his mind with thoughts that were dark, painful even to entertain. Yet they had to be faced. One thing had become clear. Clyde Keyser had sent five innocent families to be slaughtered. He had set them up as a decoy, done it so they'd draw attention to themselves and away from Angela and Amanda's drive. It had been a despicable, monstrous act. Had he done it as a favor to Angela? Did he want to brag to her later of how he had helped her make the drive without trouble?

If so, it was an act so wrong it was a sickening perversion of the term "good deed." Fargo wanted answers. He wanted to confront Clyde Keyser, to hear how he could justify sending five families to their deaths. He wanted Keyser to explain his monstrous selfishness and he turned the horse west and began to ride the open land to Almeda. It was night when he reached town but anger kept the weariness from enveloping him as he halted in front of the saloon and strode inside. His eyes swept the room, seeking out Keyser in his usual place. But he wasn't there and the madam greeted him as he approached her.

With her experienced acumen, she saw the tight line of his jaw. "Hello, big man. Something wrong?" she asked.

"Keyser, where is he?" Fargo snapped.

"He's not here. He's away," the woman said.

"Where?"

"Didn't tell me. He left a few days ago," the madam said.

Fargo's thoughts leapfrogged. Doc Carter was close with Keyser. Maybe he'd have answers. "Where's Doc Carter?" he asked.

"Haven't seen him for a few days, either. He might

have gone off with Clyde. They were together, last time I saw them," the woman said.

"Together," Fargo echoed and she nodded. He felt her words creeping into him, each opening a new door, injecting things he hadn't contemplated. Suddenly there were new intimations, new possibilities raised, and none of them pleasant to think about. Perverted good deeds, already cloaked in darkness, took on new Machiavellian proportions.

He nodded to the woman and strode from the saloon. He'd pursue the new suspicions that pulled at him, unformed and unclear, yet made of shadows that beckoned with a terrible power. Outside, he pulled himself onto the Ovaro and rode from Almeda, kept riding onto the prairie until the body demanded he halt. He bedded down on the open prairie, sleep a restless blanket until he finally succumbed to exhaustion.

6

He rode the prairie again when morning came, passing the eight trunks which, from a distance, could have been so many strange headstones. And almost were, he thought to himself. He held a nice, steady pace. There was no need to push the horse. Large herds of cattle moved slowly. He'd catch up to them well before they reached Dodge. He spent another night sleeping on the open prairie before, late the next day, he came within sight of the herd. He skirted the edges of the mass of white-faced cattle, saw nothing to indicate there'd been trouble, the hands in place doing their tasks.

Angela and Amanda rode at the head of the herd, not far from each other. They turned as he rode up from behind them. Both stared at him, astonishment wreathing their faces. Angela was first to shake off her surprise, sent her horse leaping toward him and leaned from the saddle to brush his cheek with a quick kiss. But a tiny frown stayed on her face. "This is a surprise," she said. "I expected you waiting and thinking about my return."

"Got tired doing that," he said as Amanda came over.

"What happened to tracking down silver smugglers?" she asked, as much coolness as curiosity in her face.

"Got tired of doing that, too," he said calmly. Amanda took in his answer, wariness in her face.

"You going to ride with us?" Angela asked.

"Right to Dodge," Fargo said cheerfully.

"Wonderful," Angela said, but the little furrow still touched her brow. He cast a glance at Amanda. She masked her thoughts with guarded coolness.

"Run into any trouble?" Fargo questioned as Angela and Amanda swung in beside him.

"None," Angela said.

"Let's see it stays that way," Fargo said. "Mind if I ride point for you?"

"Of course not. We've a couple of days to go yet," Angela said.

"Be back by night, 'less something sends me back earlier," Fargo said and put the Ovaro into a trot. He set out across the prairie, waved to a pair of cowhands as he passed, and was soon beyond sight of the cattle. He slowed, and scanning the land, saw low rolling hills begin to form at the far edge of the plains. A handful of unshod Indian pony prints caught his eye but that was to be expected and Indians didn't rustle cattle. He was standing, scanning the horizon, when he heard the hoofbeats behind him. He turned to see Angela ride up. He dismounted and she swung from her horse and her lips were on his at once, clinging, high, round breasts pressing into his chest.

"Have you really stopped looking for the silver?" she asked, pulling away.

He chose his words carefully. "Never been one to waste time on a trail I can't follow," he said.

"That's good thinking," she agreed. "But you could've just waited for me to get back."

"Coming after you is better," he said with a smile.

"We'll have to be careful. We can't get away alone out here on the prairie and Amanda's going to watch us like a hawk," Angela said.

"That's for sure," he said. "She takes being protective seriously."

"Yes, so I'll be going back now. Don't want to make her more suspicious than she already is. I just wanted a moment alone with you," Angela said.

"There'll be time when we get to Dodge," Fargo said.

"Yes, soon as we sell the herd and I get a day's rest," Angela said. She blew him a kiss as she rode away, all compact curves in the saddle. He rode on slowly, exploring and scanning the land again, and finally turning back as day drew to an end. He saw the small campfire that had been built as he arrived back at the herd, unsaddling the Ovaro and setting out his bedroll. Amanda strolled to him and handed him some strips of beef jerky.

"We brought along extra," she said.

"Obliged," he said and sat down near the remains of the fire. She lowered herself alongside him and he saw the faint smile touch her lips, amusement dancing in her brown eyes as she studied him.

"Why are you really here?" Amanda asked, surprising him with the question. Again, he chose words with care.

"Told you, got tired chasing after nothing," he said.

"And you never waste time on a trail you can't follow, according to Angela."

"That's right," he nodded.

The amusement continued to dance in her eyes. "Only that's a crock of shit," she said almost sweetly and he let himself look hurt. "It's not you, Fargo," she said. "You're not the kind to give up, walk away from a job because it's tough."

He allowed his own smile to answer. "Think you know that, do you?" he said.

"I'm sure of it," she answered.

"You've other reasons for me being here?" he pushed at her.

"Not yet, none that I'm sure of yet," she said. "Maybe you're wanting Angela too much but I'm not settling on that."

"Suspicion isn't becoming," he remarked.

"No, but it's true often enough," Amanda returned. "I just know one thing. Whatever your reason, it's not the one you gave."

He smiled as he swore silently at her intuitiveness. "You're being suspicious again," he said.

She returned his remark with a smile that held entirely too much wisdom and he swore again as she strolled away. It would be nice to trust her, he realized, and he didn't exactly distrust Amanda. Yet she had shown that she was filled with her own complexities, and complexities made for unknown motives. Trusting her, or anyone, would have to wait. The dark currents that had brought him here forbade trust in anyone for now.

When the fire burned out, he undressed and stretched out on his bedroll. He pushed up on one elbow as Angela appeared. She wore a short nightgown that showed her fleshy thighs. She was carrying her blanket and put it down but a few feet from his. Her hand reached out as she lay down and closed around his. She had been beside him for but a few moments when he saw the tall figure appear, coming toward them with her blanket. A loose, floor-length cotton nightdress didn't hide the long-waisted lines of her as she sat down on her blanket. "I like this," Amanda said brightly. "We can all be cozy together." Angela pulled her hand from his and he heard the anger in her as she turned on her side.

"Sleep tight," Fargo said blandly.

"Thank you," Amanda returned. Angela's silence was loud and he smiled as he closed his eyes and let sleep take hold of him. The restlessness of the steers woke him when morning came. Angela and Amanda were still asleep as he rose, Angela half out of her blanket, one lovely thigh exposed, Amanda neatly contained inside her covers. He washed with his canteen and was saddling the Ovaro when both young women awoke. They carried their blankets to where they'd left their horses, Angela's face still sullen, he noted. They used their horses as screens to change behind and he caught snatches of conversation, anger in Angela's voice.

"You embarrassed me," he heard her hiss at Amanda.

"Nonsense," Amanda returned coolly. "You weren't embarrassed, you were disappointed."

"I don't need a damn chaperon," Angela flung back.

"Hell you don't," Amanda said and both fell silent. Fargo moved the Ovaro past them as Amanda finished putting up her hair.

"I'll be riding point again," he said.

"That'll be good of you," Amanda answered, shooting him a quick glance with an apology in it. He smiled at her and rode on, slowing to watch the cowhands prepare to move the herd. Going on, he rode north again, his eyes sweeping the land. They had crossed into Kansas, he was certain. Prairie was prairie but there were subtle changes if you knew how to read them, the grass a shade greener, richer in growth, the earth not as dry. Converging cattle prints also attested to the road to Dodge. It was midday when Angela appeared. She rode up to him and halted, sliding from her horse. He dismounted and she came to him, a pout still on her lips.

"I told you she'd watch us like a hawk. I didn't think she'd be that unsubtle," Angela said.

"The prairie's no place for being subtle," Fargo said. "Didn't bother me any."

She put her arms around him. "I've been thinking about when we reach Dodge. I've an idea," she began. "It might be best if you cut out there, let her think you're going away. You can lose yourself in Dodge."

"I'm sure," he said.

"Only you'll hole up there. Amanda will concentrate on selling the herd and I'll go do some things on my own. We'll be staying at the Dodge Hotel, as we always do. You leave me a note there telling me where you are."

"And you'll come visiting," he said.

"Soon as things settle down," Angela said. "Amanda won't know a thing."

He turned Angela's plan in his mind, and found himself nodding in agreement, but for his own reasons. She didn't know it but her plan fitted his needs perfectly, freed him to pursue the reason that had brought him here. He'd ostensibly go along with everything she'd outlined, adding his own changes.

"Sounds perfect to me," he said and received an instant hug.

"Just keep out of sight, away from the herd. She sees you she'll put two and two together," Angela said.

"Got it," he said as he gave her a hand up on her horse and she threw him a smile that was both conspiratorial and satisfied as she rode away. He climbed onto the Ovaro and rode away, returning to the herd when night fell. Once again Angela laid her blanket beside his bedroll and once again Amanda joined them. He smiled as he went to sleep and found himself admiring Amanda's unswerving goal.

When morning came, he rode with the herd and by midafternoon Dodge rose up before them. As Amanda rode at the head of the herd, Angela a few paces behind her, he dropped back when they entered town. Dodge was much as he had seen it last, only bigger, noisier, and dustier, a place that existed for the buying and selling of cattle. He stayed back, becoming unobtrusive amid the cowhands herding the steers. As most cattlemen did, they'd sent notice they were bringing in a herd and a large corral waited for them. They moved toward it through town, past other penned cattle where buyers shouted bids at sellers. The din of bellowing men and bellowing cattle filled his ears as he rode alongside one line of buildings, his eyes scanning the bustle but mostly trying to stay unseen himself.

Amanda directed the herd to a large corral at the end of town, Angela beside her as the Herefords were driven inside and the gates closed. He edged his way to the corral as Amanda, Angela beside her, surveyed her cattle. "They'll bring a good price. They didn't lose much weight on the drive," Amanda said. She had just finished the sentence when a man wearing a smartly tailored tan jacket paused at the corral. He had a hard face, Fargo noted at once, not a soft line in it, a mouth thin as a razor, and cold blue eyes.

"These your steers?" he asked.

"That's right," Amanda said.

"Name's Breyer, Jack Breyer," the man said.

"You looking to buy a herd?" Angela asked.

"You know any other reason to come to Dodge, little lady," the man said.

"Make an offer," Angela said.

"Forty-five dollars a head," Breyer said.

"You haven't looked at them. You haven't gone over one steer," Amanda said.

"I've always been partial to Herefords. Is it a deal?" Breyer said.

"Forty-five a head? It's fine with me," Angela said.

"No, no, no," Amanda cut in. "My sister's impulsive. I prefer to go slower."

"It's a perfectly good offer," Angela protested.

"I'd like to have a few others," Amanda said stubbornly, looking at the man. "We'll have some by tomorrow noon. Why don't you come back then. I won't be selling without giving you another chance. My word on it."

He shrugged. "If I'm so minded," he said and strode away. When he was down the street, Angela spun on her sister.

"Dammit, Amanda, we could've had the herd sold," she spit out.

"Never take the first offer. Pa always said that," Amanda countered.

"The hell with what Pa always said," Angela burst

out and Fargo felt a pang of surprise. "A bird in the hand is worth two you know where," she said, turned, and saw Fargo. "What do you think?" She frowned.

"I think there's something to be said for both," Fargo answered.

Angela, her face angry, spun away. "I'll get our rooms. At least something will be done," she threw at Amanda and strode away, pulling her horse along.

He looked at Amanda, who appeared unruffled. "I'll be cutting out now," he said. Amanda raised one eyebrow and he saw the skepticism in her face.

"Just like that?" she inquired, sliding the question at him.

"Never liked Dodge," he said. Her smile was chiding. She needed to add no words.

"You're being suspicious again," he said.

"You're playing with truth again," she returned calmly. Damn her, he swore inwardly. He wanted to snap back at her but he realized that'd only reinforce her feelings.

"Good luck selling the herd," he said and as he walked away from her, he could feel her eyes watch him go. The day was fading as he strolled along the street, keeping to the side, losing himself in the crowd that still filled the town. He passed the Dodge Hotel and kept going, halting at a modest, neat building that proclaimed itself the Cattleman's Inn. They had a room and he took it. Next he found a stable nearby and arranged for a roomy corner stall for the Ovaro. Returning to the inn, he stretched out on a reasonably comfortable double bed in a neat, clean room with a dresser and a big water pitcher atop it. He dozed, waiting until the night thoroughly embraced the town.

Finding Clyde Keyser if he was here would be a

difficult and delicate task, Fargo realized. The man would keep a low profile until he was ready to make his move, whatever that would be. That question was still the unanswered one. So far he had only the same suspicions he'd brought with him on the drive. But the time was at hand for them to become more, to take on form and shape. His thoughts went to Doc Carter. The man had a gambling problem. He could no more stay holed up in Dodge than a fox could stay away from a henhouse. Fargo swung his long legs from the bed and stood up. If he could find Doc Carter then Keyser was here, also. It'd be the first affirmation of the hunch that had brought him here.

The night had grown long enough for him to go out, Fargo decided, and he took to the street. Stopping a storekeeper outside a general store, he asked, "What's the best place to play a little poker?"

"The Dodge Casino, just down and off Main Street," the man said. Fargo nodded thanks and strolled down the street, found the casino, a two-story, wooden building, and stepped inside. He stayed just inside the doorway, letting his eyes take in the noisy, smoky room filled with gaming tables. His gaze traveled slowly as he scanned the players at each table. He had reached the far end of the room when he spied the tall, thin figure at a table with four other men. His lips drawing back in a grim smile, he turned and hurried from the casino.

He'd found what he wanted to find. Doc Carter was here in Dodge. So was Keyser. Confirmation that gained new strength. A first step only, he realized as he returned to his room at the inn. He lay down and reviewed his next moves. Staying out of sight was his first priority. He had to see how events transpired before he could move further and he let himself rest, waiting until the night grew deep before he rose and went into the street again. Staying along the side of the street, he saw that Dodge was still crowded, a town that stayed active longer than most. He made his way to the corral that held the white-faced steers, peering at the buildings that stood near the corral. Most were slant-roofed, of no value to him. But he spotted one that rose up only a dozen yards from the corral, the roof flat, and more important, with a stone chimney rising from it.

It would have to do but the streets were still too crowded and he walked away. He risked stopping in at the casino again. Doc Carter was still there playing poker and Fargo backed out and hurried back to his room. He set his inner alarm clock, let himself sleep, and snapped awake when time drifted to the hanging minutes just before dawn. He left the room, moving through streets that were finally empty. When he reached the house he'd decided upon, he went to the back. He found a drainpipe that ran alongside an iron cornerpost and pulled himself up to the roof as the new day crept across the sky.

Flattening himself behind the chimney, he could peer out and see down to the corral below where the Herefords jostled one another. He quietly waited, watching the town come alive as new herds arrived and new buyers took to the streets. Watching, Fargo saw Amanda arrive at the corral, then Angela joining her. Various buyers came to stop by, make offers, talk, and go their way. The Herefords drew a good number of interested bidders, he saw, but Amanda kept her promise and Jack Breyer arrived a little before noon. Watching everyone's actions and body language, it was clear that a deal was being consummated. Handshakes between Breyer, Amanda, and Angela completed the agreement and Breyer wrote a check which he handed to Amanda.

The sisters walked off together and Breyer stayed awhile, peering at the Herefords he'd bought until he, too, left. Unable to climb down the drainpipe in broad daylight without calling attention to himself, Fargo remained at his rooftop hiding place. He shifted himself further behind the chimney and waited. The afternoon had begun to wane when he heard the commotion from the corral below. He swung around, peering down to see Jack Breyer standing inside the corral with three cowhands on horseback also inside the corral. As he watched, he saw Jack Breyer begin to push his way through the steers, shouldering his way amongst them, looking at each one. Finally he halted alongside the head of one steer, motioned to the riders who maneuvered their horses forward, and cut the steer away from the others and drove it to an adjoining corral.

Frowning, Fargo watched Breyer continue to push through the cattle, selecting first one, then another, and had them driven into the adjoining corral. The process was slow as Breyer went on examining each steer, ordering certain ones herded into the next corral. A kerosene lamp was brought in as darkness fell and Breyer held it aloft in one hand as he went on examining and selecting only certain steers. Fargo watched, fascinated. He'd never seen anything quite like it and finally, the night concealing, he slid backward from the roof and lowered himself down the drainpipe. He went around to the front of the house. The hard-faced man was still selecting certain steers to be herded into the next corral. But he was almost at the far end of the herd and the adjoining corral now held probably half the steers, Fargo guessed. He stayed in the shadows and watched Breyer finish selecting the last steer, which the cowhands promptly drove into the next corral.

Breyer put down the lantern, carrying it along his leg as he left the corral. Then he strode away, the three cowhands riding behind him. The entire operation made little sense to Fargo as he stared at the steers. If the man had just wanted to divide the herd he could've done that by simply driving half the herd into the other corral. But he had carefully selected certain ones to separate from others. Why, Fargo wondered as he peered at the steers. He was no cattleman but he was no amateur, either. The steers were uniform in quality, unusually so. He could see no reason for cutting some out from others.

Amanda and Angela had sold the herd in what seemed a perfectly normal transaction, nothing unusual about the sale. So much so that Fargo had found himself wondering if his dark thoughts had been wrong, fed by his own frustrations. But now the strangeness of dividing the herd jabbed at him. Perhaps the sale had only seemed routine, the ordinary masking the unordinary. What the hell did it all mean, he asked himself, and the five families Keyser had sent to be decoy victims rose in his mind. All the very ordinary events he had seen here couldn't erase that. With a silent curse, he spun on his heel and returned to the corral.

He ducked between the rails and stepped inside with the mass of steers. He moved slowly, carefully, among the cattle. They were no mean-tempered, hair-triggered longhorns, yet they could be startled and he didn't fancy being crushed by tons of panicked beef. The moon had come up, affording more than enough light for him to see. He ran his hands soothingly over the back of the nearest steer and saw nothing about the animal that differed from the others. He was about to slide forward through two more steers when his eye caught the small nick in the steer's ear. He leaned over and examined it. No barbed-wire cut, no tear from a fence splinter but a small, neat, thin incision. His brow furrowed, he went on to the next whiteface and found that it, too, had a small incision in one ear.

The one after it bore the same mark and soon he'd found that every one of the steers had a thin incision in one ear. Jack Breyer had cut out only those cattle with the marking, it seemed. But to be sure, he ducked out of the corral, went to the first corral that held the other half of the herd, and climbed inside. Again, moving carefully, he went over the steers. None had incisions in their ears. Why had the man selected only the marked ones, he pondered, again unable to see any difference among the cattle. Finally ducking out of the corral, he strolled back to the inn, feeling not unlike a man trying to put together a jigsaw puzzle with some of the pieces missing.

The sale of the herd had seemed perfectly legitimate, he told himself again. Nothing indicated that Amanda or Angela were involved in anything. But Clyde Keyser and Doc Carter were here. They hadn't made the trip to Dodge to go sightseeing. Fargo's thoughts returned to the steers. Were the steers that bore the nicked ears the ones that had been vaccinated? Had Amanda passed that on to Breyer and the man had decided to select only the vaccinated steers?

Was the explanation that harmless? He couldn't deny the possibility. But he couldn't deny five families almost decoyed to their deaths. Too much refused to fit and the dark gnawing inside him persisted. He could continue to watch and wait, he promised himself as he reached the inn and went to his room.

He was about to open the door when he noticed the faint sliver of lamplight coming from the bottom of the doorway. He drew the Colt, used his left hand to snap open the door with a turn of the key, and swept the room with the gun raised to fire. The tall, long-waisted figure rose from the edge of the bed. "You won't need that," she said.

"I'll be damned," Fargo bit out as he kicked the door shut. "I'll be damned."

7

He saw her regard him with cool amusement, enjoying his surprise. In a black skirt and white, tailored shirt that rested lightly on her breasts, she looked regally unperturbed. "Let's play three questions," Fargo muttered. "One, how'd you find me?"

"It wasn't terribly hard. I didn't believe your story about leaving Dodge and I was right." She smiled back as he glowered at her. "I asked at each hotel and inn until I found you."

"Two, how'd you get in here?" he growled.

"Told the old man at the desk that I was your wife and had lost the key. He let me in," she said.

"The old fool," Fargo grunted. "Three, what are you doing here?"

"I think you know that," Amanda said evenly.

"Enlighten me," he said.

"Same reason you lied about leaving Dodge. Angela," she said.

"Angela," he repeated. "Protecting her again." She allowed a half shrug. "You want to keep the wrong men away from her and I'm one of them."

The cool amusement disappeared from her face as she grew instantly serious. "I want to keep her from getting hurt," Amanda said.

"You think that would happen if I had her," he said.

"Eventually," Amanda said. "Oh, you'd do wonderful things for her, for any woman, I imagine."

"Do I smell a compliment?" he put in.

"A statement," she said. "But you're not going to become a rancher, stay with her, take care of her, be what she needs." She paused and his silence was an answer.

He regarded her for a long moment. "What are you saying, exactly?" he asked.

"Leave her alone. Back away from her, no matter how much she wants you. It'll be best for her," Amanda said.

He let a wry smile edge his lips. "You're asking me to go against my principles," he said.

"Such as?"

"Never refuse a free drink or a willing woman," he said blandly.

"I wouldn't think of having you go against your principles," Amanda said, sarcasm in every word. "I'll make you an offer to soften the pain."

"I'm listening," he said, felt the surprise sweep through him as she slowly undid the top button of her shirt, then the next, went on to the third, and halted. He frowned at her. "You're real serious about protecting her," he said.

"Made a promise. I keep promises," Amanda said, waiting as he studied her. "Deal?" she asked, finally.

"You can button up," he said. "Sorry, no deal."

A mixture of emotions ran through her face, surprise, hurt, chagrin, disbelief, all settling into resentment. "Why not? Am I that unappealing?" she flung at him.

"No, on the contrary," he said.

"Then why?"

"Principles, again," he said.

"Which one now?" she sneered.

"Stay away from actresses," he said.

She looked away, said nothing for a long moment. Finally she brought her eyes back to him, lifting her chin with a kind of defiance. "What if I said I wouldn't be acting?" she asked.

He studied her, saw honesty edged with stubbornness. "That'd put a different face on it," he told her.

"Am I surprising you?" she asked.

"Only the last thing you said," he answered, matching her honesty.

"Didn't plan saying it," she admitted. "But they weren't just words." Her fingers went to the fourth button of the shirt, opened it, did the same with the last, and the shirt fell open and he caught a glimpse of the edges of the longish breasts. Wriggling her shoulders, she shrugged the garment from her and he took in creamy mounds that hung in long, lovely curves, growing beautifully full at the bottom, where they swelled deliciously. A delicate pink nipple topped each, blending in with a matching areola with sweet seamlessness. Nice shoulders were rounded and broad, her long waist narrow.

She pushed skirt and half-slip from her as she pulled off her clothes, folding herself onto the bed, narrow waist joining narrow hips, the flatness of her abdomen entirely in keeping with the sinuousness of her body. Yet for all her long figure, she was no delicate wraith, a kind of very real strength emanating from her. Almost out of place, a very dense, very black triangle beckoned with its own invitation, as if demanding to be touched, explored, pressed, a kind of oasis of villous pleasure. Long, cream white thighs moved down from the point of the black triangle, all part of her flowing loveliness. She pulled a hairpin from atop her head and a cascade of soft brown hair tumbled down to frame her face. Suddenly her patrician coolness had a new, soft warmth that gave her beauty new dimensions.

He brought his lips to hers and pressed gently. He felt the stiffness of her, pressed harder, and her mouth relaxed, softening under his. Moistness came to her lips, a harbinger, and he felt her tongue emerge, tentatively at first, then with an eager boldness, circling his mouth, reaching deeper. "Oh, oh yes," she murmured as her hands dug into his shoulders. He let one hand move down, across thin, prominent collarbones, down to one longish breast and Amanda gasped at once. He cupped its softness and felt her respond. "Yes, oh, nice . . . nice," she murmured as she lifted and pressed her breast upward into his palm. His thumb circled the delicate pink areola, passing over the seamless tip and she cried out, her torso twisting with pleasure now permeating all of her.

He brought his lips down, took in her breast, drawing it in deeply and caressing the soft-firm tip with his tongue. He listened to Amanda's moans grow stronger, hardly pausing for breath. He was staying with her, savoring the soft touch of her in his mouth when he felt her long legs moving up along his waist, rubbing against him, not unlike a fly rubbing its legs together. "Please, please, more, more," Amanda murmured and he reached down, running one hand over her flat abdomen, circling the tiny indentation, sliding down further, pushing into the black, bushy nap. "Oh, oh, God," Amanda cried out, lifting her hips. He felt the rise of her Venus mound, the soft-firm rounded peak, and enjoyed the feel of her filamentlike hairs that entwined themselves between his fingers. He slid his hand down again to the very point of the dense triangle and suddenly Amanda half turned and her hands were holding his face.

She peered at him, her eyes glowing with an almost wild, dark light, something between desire and fear, as if she were searching for reassurance, not from him but from herself. With an explosion of forces she had to answer even as she cast aside understanding, she flew at him and lifted herself, smothering his face with her breasts, first one then the other as sharp little cries came from her. He spun her onto her back, touched down below the bushy triangle, and felt the warm wetness of her inner thighs. "Oh, God, oh, God, yes, yes," Amanda gasped. "Touch me, hold me, take me, give me." He slid his hand upward, touched the excruciating softness of inner lips turned upward, waiting, wanting, and he heard her gasp become a scream of pure delight.

He held her, careful little motions, strokes of tenderness and wanting and she half cried, half gasped. He brought himself to her, his own throbbing desires touching against her pubic mound, her thigh, pushing forward to touch the dark, wet portal. Amanda's fingers scratched down his back and she raised her long legs, closing them around his hips, the body offering its own entreaties. He felt the wildness coursing through her as once again, her legs rubbed up and down against him. When he slid forward, into the honeyed palace, her scream spiraled upward, hanging in the air, a paean to ecstasy.

"Oh, God, so good, so good," she murmured and

thrust upward to meet his pulsating warmth. She was suddenly transformed into a creature of total abandon. No cool containment now but an explosion of pure desire with nothing held back. She pulled his mouth down to one long breast and thrust it at him as low moans rose from her. He slowly slid deeper into the sweet warm tunnel. He let her set the pace and lost himself in the total, consuming pleasure of the feel of her around him, sensations beyond words, beyond anything but absorbing. Her body began to quicken, responding to the uncontestable drive of the senses and he heard a kind of fright come into her gasps. "No, oh, no," he heard her cry, and then, "Yes, oh yes, yes, yes, yes." Suddenly she was driving hard against him, hurling her moistness into him, answering a command she could neither slow nor turn back.

He felt his own body keep pace with her as she screamed and clutched at him. He was on a runaway carousel of the senses, one with her, faster and faster, a whirling roulade of ecstasy choreographed by Eros. It was with the suddenness that is never really sudden that she exploded, her hips lifting, long legs tightening, all of her consumed with sweet spasms. He felt himself lifted with her, joining in the shattering instant that was never long enough. His face buried into her breasts, he felt the dampness of her as she clung to him, quivering, trembling, tiny sounds falling from her lips. He heard the long, high cry break off, despair intruding on pleasure, and she fell back onto the bed with him. "No, no . . . more, oh, please more," he heard her gasp, the eternal conflict of that eternal moment when forever was only a moment.

Finally, her quivering ceased, not slowly, but abruptly, like a water faucet turned off. She fell back and stared up at him. He rose on one elbow, enjoying the languorous loveliness of her as a small, pleased smile edged her lips. "Think I was acting?" she slid at him.

"No." He smiled. "You can't disguise the real thing."

She drew his hand down to rest on one delicate pink nipple and a furrow of thought pressed into her brow. "What is it?" he asked.

"I had it all planned and now everything's different," she said and he waited. "When I first came here I had it planned that when we finished you'd leave, go your way. And now I don't want that. All I want is for you to stay, to be with you again."

"That can be arranged," he said.

"You arranged to meet Angela, didn't you?" she asked.

"I'm supposed to get in touch with her," he admitted. "But not now, of course. I keep my deals."

Her eyes probed. "Is that all it is?" she questioned.

"Now I'd be acting if I said that," he answered and satisfaction touched her eyes. "Angela finds out, she won't be happy with either of us, especially you," he added.

"Angela's never happy with me. This'll give her another reason. Maybe it'll be the best thing for her. Maybe it'll slow down that impulsiveness of hers."

"You're going to have to stop being her protector one of these days," he told her. "Maybe this is the time."

She thought about his words. "No, not yet. Unless I see a real change in her," Amanda said. "Besides, you do something for a lot of years you can't just turn it off."

124

"That's a good excuse for not wanting to," he said.

She peered at him. "You said that once before. I think maybe you had hold of something, but not anymore, not now."

"Why not now?"

"Maybe I was all held back, maybe even secretly jealous. But not after tonight," she said, bringing his face to hers, caressing his lips with hers. Finally she rose and reached for her clothes. He enjoyed the beauty of her as she dressed, breasts moving gently in unison, her long figure a thing of sinuous loveliness. "When do I see you again?" she asked as she buttoned the shirt.

His own uncertain plans flooded back over him. "I'll come calling when you get back to the ranch," he said. "When will that be?"

"We'll stay in Dodge another day or so," Amanda said. "Then be on our way."

The frown stayed off his face but with an effort. "Thought you'd finished all your business here," he remarked evenly.

"Might do some shopping, pick up some clothes," Amanda said and he grimaced silently. He wanted to trust in her, ask questions. Yet there was too much still hanging, too much that needed explaining. With Angela, she was part of the puzzle. But a totally innocent part? Was she staying to go shopping or for another reason? He wanted to believe her, believe the best of both of them. But long ago he'd learned that believing can be a road with a bitter ending. He'd not take it, he knew, no matter how much he wanted to. Right now, Amanda was convinced his coming to Dodge had been because of Angela. He'd leave it at that.

She clung to him at the door for a moment longer.

"I'll be waiting back at the ranch," she said. "More than I've ever waited for anything."

"I'll be there soon," he said. She kissed him and hurried out without looking back. She had become the more complex of the two, he decided. Angela's impulsiveness was much more simple; everything was on the surface with her. He returned to the bed, still warm with the smell of her, and closed his eyes to embrace sleep, a poor substitute for Amanda.

8

He swore when he awoke. He'd let himself over-sleep, the town already bustling and very awake. He washed and dressed and went out. He'd wanted to climb onto the roof and take up his watch again but that was out of the question now. Too many people on hand to see him. He'd try melting into the crowds, he decided, and keep watch on the corral as best he could and hope he remained unseen. After coffee and a sweet roll he moved down the street, staying against the building line. He knew he was not being too successful in trying to seem small and inconspic-uous. He cut back behind the buildings and came out again when he reached the corrals and drew to an abrupt halt.

The second corral with the vaccinated steers stood empty, the first one still filled with Herefords. He stared for a moment, transfixed, surprise and alarm gathering inside him. Pushing his way forward, he reached the corral and went to the far end. His eyes swept the ground and he saw the prints where the herd had been moved out. "Damn," he swore as he leaned down to feel the ground with the prints. The soil was still warm, the upturned ridges crumbling at his touch. The steers hadn't been driven from the corral more than a few hours earlier. He turned and hurried back through town to the stable. In minutes, he was riding the Ovaro back through the crowded main street of Dodge, past the corral, and out of town.

The trail was easy to pick up and he followed. The herd had made better time than he'd expected and it was into the afternoon when he saw the dust cloud ahead. The terrain had turned from flat rangeland into gentle hills with thick stands of shadbush, iron-wood, and bur oak. He steered the horse into a long line of oak that let him follow the herd and stay out of sight, slowing when he drew closer to the cattle. He saw the herd being turned to go into a white-fenced corral with a small house behind it. The line of oak led close to the corral and he moved forward in the tree cover, counting some eight hands driving the herd. He recognized two as being among those who had been on guard at the barn in Almeda. Another rider came into view and he saw Jack Breyer's hard face.

The man halted and watched as the steers were driven into the corral, which was filled almost to capacity. When the steers were corralled, the men dismounted, drew rifles, and took up positions surrounding the corral while Breyer went into the house. Fargo frowned as he dismounted. He stayed inside the oak and lowered himself to the ground. Once again, he'd wait and watch and once again little made sense to him. The man had bought a whole herd, why had he only taken half with him? Had he decided to take only the ones that had been vaccinated. But that would mean a tremendous per-head loss and Jack Breyer didn't seem a man cavalier about losses.

Then, those who bought cattle in Dodge were quick to ship them out to their customers. They didn't drive them to an isolated corral. It didn't fit. The strange echoes of Almeda persisted. He saw the day beginning to fade, shadows spreading over the land, when the two riders came into sight. Fargo's eyes stayed on them, saw them take form and become Clyde Keyser and Doc Carter. A kind of grim satisfaction pushed at him, vindication seemed to take shape. He leaned forward as Jack Breyer came from the house to greet Keyser and Doc Carter as they dismounted.

"Any trouble?" Fargo heard Keyser ask.

"Some," Breyer said. "Angela Carter came by as we were starting to move the herd out. She just watched but then the other one showed up."

"Amanda?" Keyser said.

Breyer nodded, his hard face growing harder. "She had a lot to say, all kinds of questions, became a real pain in the ass."

"That's like her," Keyser said as Doc Carter looked on.

"She wanted to know why we were taking only half the herd, where we were going, suspicious as all hell," Breyer said. "Didn't like it, didn't like it at all."

"What'd Angela do?" Keyser asked.

"She just sort of stood there and looked uncomfortable," Breyer said. "But I didn't like the way the other one was acting. I'm wondering what she knows."

"She doesn't know shit. She's just nosy and difficult," Clyde Keyser said.

"I didn't want to take any chances. I invited them both to come visit us," Breyer said.

"What the hell for?" Keyser snapped.

"I was afraid she might come following, snooping, show up when we didn't want her so I decided it'd be best to bring her here. I had to invite both, of course," Breyer said.

Keyser frowned in thought for a moment. "Maybe that's best," he agreed. "We have things in hand that way. When do you expect them?"

"Figured they'd be here by now," Breyer said.

"All right, post men out to watch for them, bring them in. Meanwhile, we'll go inside," Keyser said and the two men went into the house while Breyer hurried to the guards at the corral. He returned in moments and went into the house. When darkness fell, two of the guards rode out onto the plain. Fargo turned over what he'd heard in his mind, an exchange that disturbed him for reasons he couldn't define. Words that said more than they said, he frowned, sentences made of shadows. Fargo inched forward in the darkness, as far as he dared. Dropping the pinto's reins over a branch, he knelt on one knee. It was only a few moments later when he saw three figures leave the house and walk to the corral.

Jack Breyer was first, carrying a kerosene lamp. Doc Carter followed him, carrying his little black doctor's bag, and Clyde Keyser followed carrying a suitcase. Fargo watched the strange little procession, lingering on Doc Carter and his black bag. More vaccinations? Fargo murmured silently. That didn't make any damn sense, he answered himself. The three men passed two of the guards and went into the corral, Breyer holding the lantern aloft.

But the diffused light was but a small glow amid the crush of the big Herefords. The moon had ceased to cooperate, hiding behind a fairly thick cloud cover. From where he crouched, he could see only the dark mass of cattle. The three men were not idly moving amid the steers. The glow of the lantern halted, staying in place for what Fargo estimated to be almost ten minutes before moving. It halted again, staying in place another ten minutes. Fargo's lips became a thin line. All the questions that had brought him here were being answered inside the corral, he was certain. It was happening in front of him and he couldn't see. But he had to see, he told himself. He couldn't let this moment slip away and everything he'd come for elude him.

He left the safety of the trees and dropped into a crouch as he moved forward on steps silent as a cougar on the prowl. The six guards at the corral were shadowed figures but he could see that they were relaxed, standing in place as they casually peered into the night. Two were posted at the front of the corral, another two at the far side, one at the rear, and one on the side facing him. Dropping to the ground, Fargo began to crawl forward, aware that the guard was bound to see him if he remained on his feet. He inched his way across the ground and approached the rifle-bearing figure from the side. He'd railed at the lack of moonlight but now he was grateful for it and he was not more than a foot from his quarry when he saw the man straighten up and peer into the night.

The guard's instincts had alerted him. In the mysterious ways that go beyond seeing, hearing, or smelling, he had become aware of another presence. But instinct had its weak places. He peered out into the distance and not at the danger at his feet. Carefully, silently, Fargo drew the Colt from its holster and turned it so he gripped it by the barrel. With the lightninglike speed of a diamondback's strike, he leaped upward and smashed the butt of the revolver into the man's jaw. Following through, he caught the man and his rifle before either could fall to the ground. Lowering the figure silently to the ground, he emptied the rifle and placed it alongside the guard. He couldn't carry him away without being seen and dragging him noiselessly was out of the question. Glancing at the guard, Fargo decided he'd stay unconscious long enough and left him where he lay. He'd no choice, he thought unhappily.

Ducking between the fence rails, Fargo stepped inside the corral, brushed against a big steer instantly, and drew back as the animal made a sound. The glow of the lantern was unmoving, a dozen yards away, and Fargo slid his way between steers as he crept closer to the light. The three figures took shape in the lamp's light and Fargo halted at the sight of Doc Carter bent over, plunging a hypodermic needle into the underside of the steer under the base of its chest. Folds of skin hung loosely there and as Fargo watched, Doc Carter straightened up, waited some five minutes, and then brought a scalpel from his little black bag. Bending down again, he cut a thin, straight line into the skin at the base of the steer's chest, reached fingers into the opening, and drew out an oilskin packet some six inches long.

He handed Keyser the pack and the man opened it and poured the contents into one hand. In the lamplight's glow, Fargo saw the bright glint of silver in the man's hand. Keyser put the pieces of silver into the suitcase and the three figures moved on to the next steer. Fargo crept forward with them, dropped to one knee behind a Hereford's rump and watched the same process repeated again. Carter injected the steer's underside with the needle, waited another four minutes, and the made his incision in the loose skin at the base of the animal's chest. Reaching fingers into the incision, he drew out another packet wrapped in thin oilskin and handed it to Keyser, who emptied it at once. Fargo watched Keyser pour the small pieces of silver into the suitcase.

Fargo's thoughts sorted it out quickly. Doc Carter and Keyser were reversing what they had done in Almeda inside the guarded barn. There, Doc Carter had injected the steers but not to vaccinate them. There had never been any vaccination. The hypodermic needle contained a painkiller, a local anesthetic, probably morphine. It let him make the small slit in the loose skin beneath the animal's chest and put in the oilskin packet. A few quick stitches had sewn the incision closed and the steer was let out the rear of the barn. Each Hereford carried a packet of silver, two hundred thousand dollars worth of silver shipped by steer, carriers completely undetected and completely unsuspected.

Fargo found himself admiring the brilliance of the scheme. Frank Bannister, and all the other searchers, were certain the silver was being smuggled by wagon. It was both the logical and reasonable assumption. Frank Bannister's people had only searched. Others had ruthlessly killed in their efforts. But they'd all been wrong. Cattle, not wagons, carried the silver, and suddenly a lot of the missing pieces were appearing and falling into place. But he'd sort them out later. Now he had to get out of the corral so he'd be alive to tell what he'd learned. As Doc Carter went to the next steer, Fargo began to back between the big Herefords. He was halfway across the corral, the side rails through which he'd entered in sight, when all hell broke loose.

A steer near him suddenly backed, startled by something. Its huge bulk smashed hard into him and he felt himself going down. His sharp cry of pain and surprise was an automatic reaction, happening too quickly to pull back. But it cut through the night, he knew. He tried to get one leg up to prevent going down altogether and inadvertently kicked the next steer. The steer spun its rump around, slammed into him sideways, and this time he had no way to prevent falling. He felt himself pitching headfirst to the ground. He hit the hard earth, rolled himself into a ball as powerful, deadly hooves pounded the ground on both sides of him.

At his first cry of pain, Breyer had lifted the lantern high and now Fargo saw the glow spread out and sweep over where he tried to hide. "Over there," he heard Breyer shout. Avoiding hooves, Fargo straightened out, rose, and darted around the rear of another steer. "There . . . get him," Breyer called out. Fargo spied an opening and flung himself through it, swerving past another steer. The cattle were aroused, all milling and jostling as he ran for the fence. He glimpsed three of the guards converging on the fence, also, but he kept on. It was be captured or be trampled by the steers. He chose capture as the lesser of two evils. One could escape from capture but not from being ground into the soil.

Almost falling again as another steer sideswiped him, he saw the three guards had reached the rails, rifles raised and aimed at him. Clyde Keyser's voice cut through the bellowing cattle. "No. Jesus, don't shoot," Keyser shouted, alarm curling through his cry. Fargo halted, realizing the fear in Keyser's command. A shot would trigger the cattle into a stampede, the confined mass of them erupting in panic. The corral fences would never hold against the massed weight of the frightened steers. Tons of bone, muscle, and power would sweep them aside as if they were made of so many matchsticks. Fargo felt the wry smile cross his face.

If the cattle stampeded, they'd plunge forward first, the tons and tons of them smashing into the front rails of the corral. Desperate times bring desperate measures. He grunted as he drew the Colt and took aim at the three guards at the rail. He fired as he ran and one of the guards flew backward, clutching his shoulder as he fell. Fargo both felt and heard the steers erupt, a collective bellow, and then the huge mass of bodies rising upward as they plunged forward. A rush of air swept past him, catching at him and sending him stumbling sideways. He heard Breyer's voice. "Jesus, this way," the man shouted. Fargo was on one knee as he reached the fence. He started to bring the Colt up for another shot when the side rails tore away, pulling down as the front of the corral collapsed. The pounding of hooves rose up in back of him, the steers in full stampede, obliterating the corral fence.

Fargo tried to bring the Colt up again but saw the rifle stock come smashing down. He tried to pull away but the blow caught him alongside the temple. He went down as a wave of pain shot through him. When he tried to grab at the man's legs, another blow from the rifle hit him squarely this time. A gray curtain swept over him, cattle, men, fences, everything vanishing as the world disappeared. He lay still, unconscious, fingers curling into a useless fist.

9

The world returned as if it had been a dream, probing dimly into his subconsciousness. His eyelids flickered at the yellowish glow of the lamplight. He blinked, pulled his eyes open, and pain stabbed through him as he shook his head. But he forced himself to focus and a room took shape. He was in the house. Automatically, he felt the emptiness of his holster as figures took shape inside the room. Clyde Keyser materialized first, then Doc Carter, and one of the guards holding a rifle. They watched as Fargo pulled himself up and fell into a hard-backed chair.

"Goddamn son of a bitch," Clyde Keyser snarled at him.

Fargo took a moment to let everything that had happened rearrange itself in his mind. The last thing that asserted itself before the rifle butt had descended was the mass of cattle storming out of the corral. A wry smile touched his face as he peered at Clyde Keyser. "The best-laid plans gone sour. Must be frustrating. Two hundred thousand dollars stampeding all over Kansas," he said.

He held his smile as Keyser struck him across the face. "Bastard," the man shouted at him, then stepped back and composed himself. "The boys are out chasing them down now. It'll take us a few days but we'll round them up," he said.

"Maybe half of them," Fargo remarked.

"It won't matter to you. You're a dead man, Fargo," Keyser shouted. Fargo shrugged. His Colt was stuck in Keyser's belt. He didn't reply but he knew that given enough time, Keyser could round up a good portion of the steers. Still, there'd be enough that got away. Small triumphs, Fargo thought, but it was the best he could salvage from all that had happened. Sudden noise at the door drew everyone's attention and Fargo watched as the two guards entered with Amanda and Angela. Amanda in jeans and her tailored white shirt, Angela in a denim skirt and sweater that showed off her high, curvaceous bustline. A frown of consternation on Amanda's brow deepened when she saw Fargo. He saw surprise but nothing more than that on Angela's round face.

"What are you doing here?" Amanda asked of Fargo.

"Visiting. Social call. Of sorts," he answered blandly.

Her eyes went to Keyser. "What the devil's going on? We saw the Herefords running all over the place," she said.

Keyser motioned to Fargo. "His goddamn fault," the man barked. Amanda stared at Fargo, her brow furrowed. Fargo glanced at Angela and saw surprise turning into impatience.

"His fault?" she said to Keyser. "They were your responsibility."

"What about Jack Breyer? He bought them from us." Amanda asked.

"Be quiet," Angela hissed and Fargo saw Amanda's eyes grow wide with surprise.

"We'll get them back," Keyser said to Angela, apology in his voice. "Most of them," he added.

"Most of them's not good enough," Angela said, her voice made of ice. "You said there'd be no problems."

"I didn't figure he'd show up," Keyser said, gesturing to Fargo.

"Will somebody please explain all this to me," Amanda cut in, her eyes going from Keyser to Angela then holding on Doc Carter. "What's he doing here?" she asked.

Fargo uttered a grim laugh inside himself as the conversation between Keyser and Jack Breyer swam into his mind, taking on a new message with new meaning. The unsaid words that had bothered him were suddenly blazingly clear, all but shouting as they leaped in his mind. *She don't know shit,* Keyser had said to Breyer's question. *She don't know shit.* Not *they* don't know shit. Just *she.* Answers explode in strange ways, Fargo thought to himself. A single word that flung wide doors. Angela felt his eyes boring into her. She looked back when she realized what she saw in the lake blue orbs.

"Got it all figured out, don't you?" she snorted.

"Pretty much," Fargo said.

"What figured out? What's going on? I want an explanation," Amanda said.

With angry suddenness, Angela reached out, grasped Amanda's wrist, and flung her into the chair alongside Fargo. "Sit down and shut up," she snapped.

Amanda stared wide-eyed at her, genuinely taken

aback. Keyser stepped forward and barked orders at the three guards. "Watch them," he said, motioning to Fargo and Amanda. "We're going out to check on how things are coming." He strode from the room with Doc Carter following on his heels. Carter passed Fargo, spearing him with a long glance. Fargo saw that the weakness in the man's face had taken on a new cast. A kind of eager cruelty had replaced weakness. He and Keyser went out and Fargo's eyes found Amanda. She was staring at Angela.

"What's it all mean? Talk to me, Angela," she said. "I don't understand any of this."

Angela ignored her and stared across the room, her lips drawn in tightly. Fargo spoke up, his voice calm, almost gentle. "Frank Bannister's silver is inside your steers," he said. "Thanks to Doc Carter's skills." He paused as Amanda stared at him. "They're the most valuable damn Herefords in existence," he added, looking at Angela. "Angela knows. She's been part of it from the very beginning." Angela stared back at him, her face impassive, but fury in her eyes.

"You didn't figure it," she hissed.

"You're right. You were very good," he said. "But it all fits into place, now. I missed a lot, misread a lot, including that first night when you went back to the herd trapped in the sinkhole. All that concern and sympathy for the helpless steers. A terrific performance, only it was just that, I know now. Hindsight is wonderful. You went back because you figured if the wolves tore apart the steers you might be able to retrieve a few packets. I came by and got in the way of that."

"Getting in the way is a bad habit," Angela returned coldly. "It's going to end, now."

"Angela, what are you saying?" Amanda interrupted, still unwilling to believe the worst.

"You're so goddamn naive, Amanda," Angela said with a sneer.

"She's not naive. You're good at wearing your mask," Fargo cut in. "You fooled me and I'm sure as hell not naive. You came up with one good reason after another to keep me away from her, all little masterpieces of plausibility. The only thing you could never thoroughly mask was your resentment of Amanda."

"You're forgetting something. Our night. I didn't wear a mask. I enjoyed every fucking minute, to put it literally," Angela said with amusement. Fargo cast a quick glance at Amanda. Her lips fell open as she stared at him and let Angela's words sink in. Her explosion of fury caught him off guard, her slap smashing across his face.

"You bastard," she shouted. "You lying bastard."

He glanced at Angela as she looked on, surprise sliding across her face, then realization. "Don't tell me," she said, her eyes turning to Amanda. "I'll be damned." Amanda's face turned a deep pink. "Miss Proper got laid," Angela chortled. "Miss buttoned-up unbuttoned. What do you know? Surprises never end."

"Must you be so crude?" Amanda threw back, her face still pink.

"You won't have to worry about that anymore. It's over. You're over, Amanda," Angela said.

"What do you mean?" Amanda asked.

"The last condition in Pa's will. You'll be filling it," Angela said smugly and Fargo saw Amanda glance at him.

"What's she talking about? What last condition?" Fargo asked her.

"I didn't mention it. Didn't seem important," Amanda said. "If either of us leaves, walks away from the ranch, everything goes to the other."

"And you're leaving, sister dear. You're walking out never to show up again. In sixty days, as per Pa's will, Judge Darian will sign and seal everything over to me," Angela said.

Amanda stared at her, incomprehension still in her face. "You're going to kill me?" she said.

"Let's just say you're going to leave forever," Angela answered.

"It's a little late for delicacy," Fargo commented.

"Shut up," Angela snapped, turning to the three guards. "I'm going to put the horses away. Watch them. They get away and it'll be your heads, I promise you."

"They won't," one of the men said as Angela strode from the house. Fargo eyed the three guards. All three had their rifles pointed at him and Amanda. He seemed to relax as he leaned back in the chair, but his thoughts raced. He had one card left to play. The thin-bladed, double-edged throwing knife was still in its holster around his calf. Only he knew it was there. He'd have to find a time to use it but this wasn't it. He'd only have one chance and he had to make it the right one. If he chose the wrong time, they'd find out about the knife and the last chance for freedom would be gone.

He glanced at Amanda. Outwardly, her face seemed calm. Inside, she was a churning cauldron of emotions, he knew, foremost among them incredulity, bitterness, betrayal. Everything she had lived for and by had shattered around her. Feeling his eyes on her, she looked up and he saw the pain in them. He had no great and profound words for her but she needed something to pierce the dark, introspective bitterness that could make her resigned to her fate. A dose of wry truth might snap her out of it, he decided. "Know what I think?" he asked and she glanced at him. "I don't think Angela needs a helluva lot of protecting," he said mildly.

She stared at him. When she finally answered, he knew he'd broken through. "It seems not," she said. "Guess she never did."

"Your pa had her figured all wrong and took you along with him," Fargo said. "It's as simple as that."

"Maybe it is," Amanda said, nodding slowly. "Seems we've both taken different roads to come to the same place."

He wanted to offer a thread of hope but didn't dare, the three guards close enough to hear anything he said. "Win some, lose some." He shrugged.

"How can you be so casual?" she questioned, resenting his attitude.

"Practice," he said as the door opened and Angela came in followed by Keyser and Doc Carter, Jack Breyer following. All wore grim faces. "It's amazing how far a frightened steer can run," Fargo remarked airily.

"Shut your smart mouth," Keyser shot back. "We'll do better come daylight tomorrow."

Fargo saw Amanda's eyes follow Angela. "You were in it from the start. Was it your idea?" she asked.

Keyser answered. "My boys hijacked Bannister's silver. Doc Carter came up with the idea of how to get it to Dodge after we refined it. I got hold of Angela."

"I get the ranch and my share of the silver. Clyde and the others will split the rest," Angela said.

"Don't worry, we'll round up the others tomorrow," Keyser said. Fargo's laugh earned him another blow, this time from Jack Breyer.

"We'll take care of you tomorrow, too," the hard-faced man said.

"He's no problem. We shoot him and dump him somewhere, alongside a road maybe. They find him they'll just figure he took on one fight too many. Nobody'll ask anything more," Keyser said and turned to Amanda. "She's the real problem."

"That's right," Angela said. "Both of us are known all through the territory. She's found shot or knifed there's going to be a lot of questions, the kind that can backfire."

"Doc and I talked about that. He's got that solved," Keyser said.

"She won't be found," Doc Carter said. "Not so's anybody will recognize her." He paused and Fargo saw the sadistic pleasure take hold of the man's face. "I'll cut her into pieces. They might find a stray leg or an arm but they won't be able to identify anyone." Fargo felt the revulsion sweep through him as he had to keep himself from leaping at the man.

"They could identify her head," Breyer said.

"Not when I'm finished with her," Carter said. "Remember, I'm a surgeon."

Clyde Keyser looked at Angela. "It's the only way. As you said, too many people know both of you. This way she'll just disappear forever. Folks will figure what you want, that she just went off somewhere. It's the only way that can't backfire."

Angela frowned in thought for only a short moment. "Dead's dead. I guess it doesn't much matter how you get there," she said.

Amanda's voice was hoarse but he heard the terrible sadness in it. "I don't know you, Angela. I guess I never did. But there's a sickness taken hold of you. You've gone over the edge. You can't go along with this."

"Shut up. I told you, I've stopped listening to you," Angela flung back and turned to Keyser. "Your show, your call. Do whatever you have to do. I'm going upstairs and get some sleep. I'll be out at dawn rounding up steers while you take care of everything else."

"It'll be all done by the time you get back," Doc Carter said with oily promise. Angela strode from the room and Fargo heard her going up the stairs. His eyes went to Amanda. She was in quiet shock, unable to believe what she couldn't avoid believing. Fargo's hand closed over her arm and he knew it could be but a helpless gesture. Doc Carter's voice cut into his thoughts.

"Get me a lariat and one of those burlap sacks," he ordered. Breyer left and soon returned with the kind of large burlap sack used for storing grain. Doc Carter approached Amanda, took the lariat from Breyer, and began to tie Amanda, working with surgical precision. Drawing her knees up first, he tied the rope around her, drawing a line to her ankles to keep her knees bent. The next ropes went to her thighs and ran up and around her waist. Her arms next, they were tied so they were held against her body. Soon she was deftly trussed, unable to move more than fingers and toes. Fargo swore in helpless silence as he saw the fear in Amanda's eyes. "Put her in the sack, feet first," Carter ordered and Breyer began to draw the burlap sack up around her.

Carter leaned forward to Amanda. "The sack will stay on you when I begin," he said. "I'll tear open the bottom so I can get to your legs, first. I'll start from the knees down. I leave the sack on because it helps soak up blood. Then I'll go to your thighs. By then I'd guess you'll pass out."

"You're enjoying this, you sick bastard," Amanda spit at him. Carter pulled a kerchief from his pocket as Breyer brought the burlap sack up to Amanda's chest and wrapped the kerchief around her mouth and tied it. He gestured and Breyer brought the sack up around Amanda's head and tied it. Unable to move, she could have been grain inside the sack, Fargo saw.

"We'll take her in the buckboard out back, in case we run into anybody on the way. There's a nice lake north of here," Keyser said and nodded to Fargo. "Tie him good. He'll stay here till we come back for him. Arms in front of him so's he can hold onto a saddle horn." Breyer brought the lariat, tied Fargo's wrists together in front of him, then pulled his knees up before he bound his ankles. Pushing him to the floor, Breyer propped him up against the wall and checked the ropes again.

"He won't be opening these," he said.

"Let's get some shut-eye," Keyser said, walking from the room after turning the lamp down low. The others followed and Fargo was left alone. Listening to the men go their ways outside, Fargo let a long breath leave his lips. He had stayed quiet when he wanted to lash out at the men, especially Doc Carter. But his self-discipline had paid off. They had done what he hoped they would—tied his hands in front of him.

Time was running out, he knew, and he'd had no idea of how to avoid being caught again if he managed to get free.

But then, without knowing it, Doc Carter and his burlap sack had given him a plan, slender and desperate as it was. Doc Carter, a man named Giuseppe Verdi, and the strange power of memory to rise out of the past at the crucial moment. It had been an opera called *Rigoletto*, that he had happened to see in St. Louis, put on by a traveling opera company. He had been taken with the performance and the music and story had stayed with him. Now, perhaps triggered by desperation, the grim, twisted ending of the opera rose up in his mind to pull at him, memory offering a grim plan for survival. But first he had to overcome the problem of cutting himself loose. It was not impossible. He'd managed to do it before. But failure was a constant shadow, waiting for one thing to go wrong, for strength to fail, for a mistake to end all hope, for pain to defeat the spirit. And there was always time, looming over everything, taunting, mocking. He'd done it before and that meant nothing, he realized grimly.

He swung his arms over to his right leg, his wrist bonds moving his hands together. His fingers grasped the edge of his pants leg and he slowly began to lift the material. Working his fingers spiderlike, he pushed the pants leg up until it reached the leather sheath around his calf. Able to use only the ends of his fingers, he gripped the handle of the knife and began to pull it out of the leather sheath. He worked slowly, carefully, all too aware that if he dropped the knife it could skitter away beyond retrieving. Finally, he lifted the blade from the holster, holding it in his fingers as he lowered his hand until he reached the bottom of his pants. He halted, carefully turning the blade in his fingertips until it rested against the wrist ropes. Gripping the handle with his fingers, he began to saw the thin, double-edged blade against the ropes.

Able to use only maddeningly short strokes, he also found he had to stop every few minutes as his fingers cramped up and wait until they uncramped before he could go on again. The process was agonizingly slow and agonizingly painful and he cursed with each tiny, sawing motion. Minutes seemed hours, the blade making only tiny cuts in the rope, and he forced himself to ignore the pain as much as he could. He took comfort in only one thing. The lariat wasn't good imported manila hemp but an inferior low-grade sisal. Still, the hours dragged on and he lost track of time. His fingers so sore, so cramped, he could barely hold the knife any longer, he had to stop for another rest. He sat back and felt the rope loosen against his wrist. Straightening up at once, excitement surging through him, he pulled his wrists apart and the rope gave way.

Shaking off the other end of the rope, he took the knife in hand again and reveled in the three long slashes he made in the ropes around his ankles. Placing the ropes carefully on the floor, he stood up and went to the window. Peering around the edge of the worn curtain, he saw the sky beginning to lighten. In three long strides he was at the burlap sack, pulling the top open and down. Reaching in, he took the kerchief from Amanda's mouth. She stared at him and he saw despair turn into hope in her eyes. This time he didn't cut ropes but carefully untied them from around her body and helped her out of the sack. She leaned against him for a long moment. "Let's run. Let's get away from here," she murmured.

"Just running won't help any," Fargo said. "It'll get us out of here but they'll come after us as soon as they find we're gone. One horse with two riders can't out-run them. We have to buy real time to get away."

"There's no way to buy time," Amanda said.

"There's one way," he said grimly. "We've got to get them to carry out their plans. That'll give us enough of a headstart."

"Carry out their plans?" She frowned. "Impossible. They'll see we've gone the minute they come in here."

"No, not if I can do it right," Fargo said.

"Do what?" Amanda asked.

"Wait here," he said. He crossed the room and eased the door open silently and stepped into the small entranceway. He took the stairs in silent steps. Snores came from the first room and the second. The third was silent and he pushed the door open, and saw the compact figure on the cot, round, high breasts pushing upward as she slept on her back. He went to her on the balls of his feet, put one hand over her mouth. Angela's eyes snapped open at once, taking a moment to focus. She was starting to open her mouth to scream when his fist caught her on the point of the jaw. She fell back, unconscious instantly.

He lifted her, slung her over his shoulder, and carried her downstairs to the room. Amanda's eyes widened as he strode to the bag and lay Angela down. He began to tie her just the way Doc Carter had tied Amanda, the first ropes around her calves, then around her knees, her thighs next until she was bound and trussed, legs drawn up, arms to her sides, exactly as Amanda had been. He pulled the burlap sack around her, closed it over her head, and put it on the floor. "They'll take her, think it's me," Amanda said.

"That's right," he said, keeping his voice even. "My Ovaro is in that stand of oaks beyond the house. You go there and wait with him. It's heavy tree cover. You won't be seen."

"What'll you be doing?" she asked.

"Sitting right here where they left me, the ropes on my wrists and ankles, only the places where I've cut will be at the bottom where they won't see them," Fargo said. "They've got to think everything's exactly as they left it. Angela told them she'd be out first thing rounding up steers. They won't give her a second thought."

"They'll take the burlap sack and ride off with it, just as they planned," Amanda said.

"That's right," Fargo said quietly.

"Only they'll have Angela in it," she said.

He saw the turbulent emotions racing through her face, distaste, fear, and hope, everything conflicting inside her, the desperate desire to survive and the repugnance at what was entailed. "It's the only way we'll get away alive," he said quietly. She stared back. "Time's running out," Fargo said. "Leave, get to those oaks before it's daylight. There's no time to wrestle with your conscience. Go, now, dammit," he added, his voice hardening, spearing her. She turned, pain in her eyes as she slipped from the door. He went to the curtain and watched her run across the open land with the dark still covering her. She disappeared beyond his sight but on her way to the oaks.

He returned to the wall, lowered himself to the

floor, and carefully arranged the ropes, on his ankles first, then around his wrists. The day came into the room as he finished and he surveyed the bonds, satisfied that they appeared perfectly in place. Jack Breyer was first to come down, then Doc Carter and Keyser. The guards sauntered in last. All cast a glance at Fargo as they passed. Fargo watched them sullenly. "Pick her up, put her in the buckboard," Keyser ordered and three of the guards lifted the sack and carried it out. "I'll have two of the boys go chase down steers. The rest can come with us," Keyser said. Fargo did a quick count in his mind. That made six going to the lake to witness the grisly task.

Keyser paused in front of him for a moment. "You're next when we get back," he said. Fargo stayed sullen. He watched them go, his eyes hardening as he saw Doc Carter take his little black bag up, a jauntiness in his step. He was the most monstrous of them all, Fargo decided. Greed drove Keyser's ruthlessness. Opportunity fueled Breyer's callousness. But Carter was a sadist who used cruelty to mask weakness, a man who thoroughly enjoyed hurting others. If things worked out so that he could only get one of them, it'd be Doc Carter, Fargo promised himself. He waited as they left and listened to them as they hitched up the buckboard. The wagon rolled away, the riders with it. But he stayed in place until the sound of them faded away before he leaped to his feet.

He slid from the door. Carefully scanning the scene, he saw where they had fixed the corral and the few dozen steers in it. Breaking into a run, he raced across the open land to the oaks. He pushed into the trees and made his way to where he'd left the Ovaro. Amanda stood beside the horse, her eyes on him as he came up. He took the reins from the branch and motioned to her. "Let's ride. Every minute counts," he said.

"I'm not going," Amanda said quietly.

10

"You're kidding," Fargo said.

"No," she said, her face grave. "I'm going back, catch up to them. Maybe there's an extra horse in the barn. If not, I'll run."

"This is crazy," Fargo said.

"I can't let this happen to Angela," Amanda said.

"She was going to let it happen to you," he thrust at her.

"She's sick. She's gone a little crazy. That wasn't the real her."

"It's the real her now," Fargo said harshly.

"No," Amanda said with a firm shake of her head.

"Yes, dammit," Fargo threw back. "What do you expect you can do by going back?"

"Stop Doc Carter before he goes too far, throw a stone at him, anything to stop him," Amanda said. "You heard him describe how he was going to proceed, from the legs, first, then the calves. He'll have Angela dismembered before he realizes it's not me."

"Suppose you get there in time to stop him. What do you think's going to happen then?" Fargo questioned.

"They'll let Angela out of the sack."

"You think when Angela sees you, that you came

back and saved her from becoming prime cuts, she'll get all grateful and teary-eyed," Fargo said.

"Yes," Amanda said firmly. "She'll see how wrong she's been, how terrible it all is."

He swore silently. She would not or perhaps could not come to grips with the terrible enormity of Angela's acts. She couldn't accept the depths of depravity that was Angela. It was too searing, too shattering. He put gentleness into his voice. "She won't see, Amanda," he said. "She won't because she can't. She's sick. She's gone over the edge. You said it yourself and you're right."

"Maybe I'm wrong," Amanda said doggedly.

He reached out and closed a hand over her arm. "I don't like this any more than you do. But I like being alive even more."

"Being alive?" Amanda frowned. "I'd never be able to sleep again if I ran away and let Angela be dismembered. That wouldn't be alive, ever."

"It's suicide to go back. You're counting on something that won't happen," he said.

"I'm counting on the person I've known all my life coming back," she said.

"If you're wrong?" he pushed at her.

She thought for a moment and finally shrugged. "You do what you have to do. It's called keeping faith with yourself."

"It's called being stupid," he threw at her even as he understood. She couldn't do differently. It wasn't in her. Reason and logic are outside things. We acquire their persuasions. Faith and conviction are inside things, a part of us beyond touching. Rationality was never a match for emotion.

"I don't expect you to come with me," Amanda

said. "You've done all you could. I'll never forget that."

"Go back and you won't have much time for remembering," he growled, swearing inwardly as he swung onto the Ovaro. "Get the hell up here," he said. Amanda's eyes widened and then she pulled herself onto the saddle in front of him. "You're a damn fool and I'm a bigger one," he said. "But you had one thing right. You do what you have to do and I can't let you commit suicide. I want to sleep nights, too."

He put the Ovaro into a fast canter and began to make plans, as few as he had to make. He had the big Henry in his saddlecase but it was essentially a long-range weapon. It didn't allow the quickness of firing and switching targets a six-gun did. But he'd have to make do with it. But it was still one gun against six. He'd need an edge, something to give him an advantage, even one made of seconds. He was still thinking as he saw the terrain grow into gently rolling hills. Lots of tree cover, he was grateful to see, lots of hackberry, cottonwoods, shadbush, and smooth sumac.

Amanda glanced at him as his eyes swept back and forth across the distance. "Trying to find the buckboard?" she asked.

"No," he said curtly. He didn't feel kindly toward her and Amanda knew not to press. His gaze continued to sweep the terrain when he spied what he had been searching to find, the glint of blue water under the sun. He put the Ovaro into a gallop, turning into a line of hackberry that led to a large, brilliantly blue lake. He saw the buckboard just drawing to a halt at the edge of the lake. Threading his way through the trees, Fargo brought them as close as he dared on horseback. They had just unloaded the burlap sack and laid it on the ground, Doc Carter standing beside it. Two of the guards had been posted at the edges, one almost touching the trees where Fargo had dismounted.

They were taking no chances on unexpected visitors stumbling onto them. "Stay in the saddle," he said to Amanda as he pulled the rifle from its saddlecase. He wanted their attention frozen, something to surprise them, give him that precious advantage of time. He was considering how to make that happen when the question was resolved. Doc Carter opened his little black bag and took out his scalpel. He held it up to the sun, smiling lovingly at the tool. "Ride out," Fargo said to Amanda. "You came to save Angela. It's showtime." He saw Doc Carter cut open the bottom of the burlap sack right before he looked up to see Amanda riding the pinto into the open.

His astonished frown was not the only one, Fargo saw as Doc stood up and watched Amanda ride to a halt. "Surprise," Amanda said, taking in the others with a sweeping glance. Keyser looked at Breyer, then at Doc Carter, his jaw hanging open. Finally he brought his eyes back to Amanda. "I'd look inside your sack," Amanda said evenly. Doc Carter used the scalpel to slit the burlap open. He stared down at the figure inside the sack as one of the guards lifted Angela up. Severing the ropes binding her, Doc Carter helped her stand. He took the kerchief from her mouth. Fargo dropped to one knee and raising the big Henry, watched as Angela stepped forward, her eyes on Amanda. "I came back," Amanda said. "I couldn't let them cut you apart."

Fargo watched, his lips pulled back in a grimace. He desperately hoped Amanda's faith in Angela would be everything she wanted even as he knew she would receive only one more shattering blow. He cast a glance at Angela's eyes and knew pain would be Amanda's reward. "You always were a fool, Amanda. You still are," Angela spit out. Fargo tore his eyes from Amanda as her face drained of color. This was the moment he wanted. He couldn't waste it being sympathetic. He aimed, fired, and Doc Carter screamed as his hand shattered. Fargo swung the rifle and fired again, and the nearest guard spun in a half circle before he went down. Out of the corner of his eyes he saw Amanda dive from the saddle as Keyser and Breyer yanked their guns out and began firing into the trees.

But they were wild shots that whistled harmlessly past him and Fargo pressed the trigger again. Jack Breyer's hard face stayed hard even as he knew life was fleeing his body. He staggered, pitched forward to quiver for a moment on the ground, and then lay still. Fargo swung the Henry around and fired again and the other guard fell sideways and lay still. He had started to pull the trigger again when he heard Angela's voice. "One more shot and she's dead," Angela shouted. But he had fired and saw Doc Carter scream again as his other hand exploded. The man cried out in a high-pitched wail as he dropped to both knees, both bloody hands hanging limply, useless appendages now.

Fargo's eyes shifted and found Angela. She had a six-gun held to Amanda's temple, no doubt taken from the guard lying nearby. "I said one more shot and she's dead," Angela repeated.

"My finger was already pulling the trigger," Fargo said. Angela's eyes narrowed and Keyser and the last guard moved to stand behind her.

"Drop the gun and come out," Angela said.

"Let her go first," Fargo countered.

"Come out or she's dead," Angela snapped. Fargo saw sadness mix with shock in Amanda's face.

"She dies, you die," Fargo said, catching the flash of alarm in Angela's eyes. He grunted with grim satisfaction. Angela was twisted, ruthless, absolutely without morals, but she was no fanatic, willing to sacrifice her life rather than lose. The advantage had swung to him, Fargo realized. He waited and let Angela twist in her own predicament.

She wrapped one arm around Amanda's neck and started to pull her backward toward the horses. Clyde Keyser and the guard moved with her, glad to include themselves in the standoff Angela had taken. But she had backed down from an exchange of bullets, Fargo noted, and had tossed the decision to him. She reached the horses, pulling Amanda behind one as a shield while she pushed Amanda up into the saddle and swung on behind her. Keyser and the guard climbed onto their horses. "No, you can't leave me," Doc Carter cried out. "Look at my hands. I can't ride. Help me."

Angela spurred her horse forward, the six-gun held to Amanda's ribs, and Keyser and the guard raced alongside her. Fargo swore to himself. He could bring Keyser down. It was the clearest shot. But the shot could trigger a reaction in Angela, nerves setting off their own answer and Amanda would pay the price. He held back firing and watched the trio go into a gallop as they fled. The scream of pain and fury split the air and he saw Doc Carter racing at the trees, waving his bloody hands, his face a mask of insane fury. Something caught a glint of sunlight in one bloody hand and Fargo saw the scalpel held between twisted fingers. Killing Carter would be easy. It'd be doing him a favor and Fargo didn't do favors for monsters. Carter deserved something more appropriate. He deserved to live in pain and uselessness the rest of his years. He deserved his life dismembered.

Screaming, Fargo neared the trees. Carter raised one arm holding the scalpel in the bloody, shattered hand. Fargo fired, the first shot blowing apart the man's left kneecap, the second his right. As Carter pitched forward with a scream of agony another shot rang out and his shoulder exploded in a shower of bone and blood. Fargo turned away, loaded the rifle, and pushed it into its saddlecase as he climbed onto the Ovaro. He rode from the trees, sending the horse into a gallop and going after the three fleeing riders. Their tracks led up a low hill into heavy timberland and he quickly gained on his quarry, slowing as he picked up the sound of their hooves. He stayed back and let the day go into afternoon, then into the long shadows of dusk. By now they'd be letting themselves wonder if he'd decided not to pursue them. He let a thin smile edge his lips.

Dusk came, pursued only by night, and Fargo heard the sound of their hoofbeats abruptly end. They had halted and he reined to a halt. Sliding from the saddle, he began to lead the Ovaro forward on foot. Tall, thick ironwoods rose up to make the night a land of stygian blackness. He moved forward slowly, halted, letting his nostrils widen as he drew in the night scents. The tangy pungency of Resurrection spike moss came to him as it uncurled in the dampness of the night. The unmistakable dank odor of Dog Stinkhorn told him his path was strewn with old stumps and rotting wood. He made a detour and crept forward, taking in the smell of a badger nearby. The moon was rising, beginning to throw its pale light through the trees when he caught the odor he wanted to smell, the tang of horses still wet from being ridden hard.

He shifted direction, went forward another half-dozen yards, and dropped the Ovaro's reins over a low branch. Moving on alone, the moon affording a pale light, he spotted the three horses tethered together. He paused, letting his eyes search the woods to the left, then the right. He was certain they had concluded he hadn't taken after them but Angela was not one to take chances. Keyser had hijacked the silver but that had taken only guns and men. Angela had plotted the subtleties of everything that followed. She'd not grow careless now. He moved forward, one careful step at a time, pausing between each, and finally saw the figures in a loose circle on the ground. But there were only three. The fourth hid nearby, awake and on guard.

Fargo dropped to one knee and rested against the thick trunk of an old ironwood, laying the rifle at his side. He settled down and let himself doze. He woke when he heard footsteps and he peered into the woods. He saw Clyde Keyser standing, the guard walking up to him with a brief, whispered exchange. The guard lowered himself to the ground and Keyser walked into the deep shadows of the trees. They had exchanged watch shifts. Fargo glanced at the two figures asleep on the ground nearby. One had to be Angela, the other Amanda. She was no doubt tied for the night, Fargo guessed. But he saw where Keyser had gone into the trees to take up his watch and, circling the figures on the ground, Fargo moved toward the trees where Keyser had gone. He halted after a few more steps, the darkness too dense to see through.

He rested again and catnapped, his inner senses alert. He was awake when the first gray-pink light of dawn filtered through the trees. As the day grew stronger he could see the three figures on the ground and, squinting, he picked out Keyser standing not more than a half-dozen yards from him. He could pick off Keyser with one shot but he knew what the others would do. The guard would wake and take cover behind the nearest tree, ready to shoot. Angela would have her gun against Amanda at once. It would essentially be a repeat of the same standoff, with Keyser out of the picture. Fargo rose and started forward in a crouch. He didn't want to give Angela another chance at holding Amanda hostage. She'd be more on edge than the first time, her nerves already frayed. She could panic and explode in a nervous reaction to anything. Amanda would pay the ultimate price and she was the only one who didn't deserve to pay that final, irrevocable price.

He was only a few feet from Keyser, who was positioned behind one of the smaller ironwoods. He drew the thin, double-edged throwing knife from its calf-holster and saw Keyser stretch. Fargo let the blade fly and thought of five families that had been coldly, ruthlessly earmarked for death. Keyser never saw the blade that hurtled into him. He had time only to stiffen, his eyes bulging and his body trembling before it sank to the ground. But Fargo was already racing through the trees. He caught the man before he hit the ground, held him for a moment, and then lowered him silently to the mossy underfooting.

Retrieving the blade, Fargo wiped it clean on the moss, reached down, and took his Colt back from Keyser's belt. Carrying the Colt in his right hand, the rifle in his left, he moved toward the three figures just waking a dozen feet away. He saw the guard on his feet, Angela stretching and getting up and Amanda sitting nearby. Angela went to her and untied the ropes around her ankles and wrists. She took the lengths of rope with her as she walked away. Taking another few steps closer, Fargo saw Angela's six-gun in the waist of her jeans. She halted and peered into the trees. Fargo ducked behind a trunk. "Clyde?" she called. He saw her wait and begin to frown as she peered into the trees. "Clyde," she called again, her tone commanding this time. She shot a glance at the guard and Fargo saw the man shrug.

Angela frowned into the trees for another moment, suddenly exploding into action. She spun as she yanked the six-gun from her waist and rushed at Amanda, moving with an explosive speed he hadn't expected. Fargo ran forward and fired the Colt and the rifle at the same time. The guard fell back into a tree trunk as the Colt's shot slammed into him. Angela's body jerked as if she'd been yanked by invisible strings as the heavy rifle slug struck her and

Fargo heard Amanda's scream. He skidded to a halt, both guns raised to fire again. But the guard lay in a heap against the base of the tree and Angela half crawled toward Amanda, trying to bring her gun up. Fargo's finger began to tighten on the trigger of the rifle when Angela shuddered and fell forward, face-down, managing to turn on her side before she lay still.

Fargo moved forward. He halted as Amanda rose and went to Angela's still figure and knelt down beside her. He saw her reach down and run her hand gently over Angela's hair, as if she were saying good night. She kept stroking Angela's hair and rubbing the back of her hand over Angela's round cheeks. Fargo holstered the Colt, stepped forward, took Amanda's arm, and gently pulled her to her feet. He saw the wet stains on her face, then, and she turned her eyes on him. "Why?" she asked, pain and incomprehension in her eyes. "Why? Why? Why?"

He drew her to him and held her as she repeated the word, making a terrible litany out of it. "You want answers I can't give. I'm not sure anyone can," he said. "Some trees grow up straight and strong the way they ought to. Some grow up twisted and crooked. Same sun, same rain, same winds."

"There has to be something to account for it," she said.

"It's what we have, what we can give and what we can take, be it tree or flower, man or woman," he said. He led her to where he'd left the Ovaro, put her in the saddle, and rode away. She stayed silent until he halted at the corral with the steers in it.

"What are you going to do?" she asked.

"Get Frank Bannister his silver," Fargo said. "Hire

some hands in Dodge and round up the rest of the herd. I figure we can find most of them with a little time. I'll drive them back to Bannister and let him take back his silver however he wants to."

"Mind if I help? I feel I owe him that much," Amanda said.

"By my guest," he said. She agreed with a grave nod. He didn't expect her to find a smile as they returned to Dodge. She didn't find one in the days that followed, or all the way back to Frank Bannister's place where they delivered most of the herd and the silver in Keyser's suitcase. But he caught the moments of anger in her face and he picked up the sharpness she directed at him. When he finally rode back to her place, he dismounted, waiting as she paused beside him.

"I won't be forgetting the things you did. I'll always thank you for them," she said, all formal and distant.

"You always hold a grudge this long?" he asked.

"What grudge?" she returned stiffly.

"You know damn well," he said. "You know what's in your craw and I know."

Her eyes flashed, anger and hurt in their brown depths. "You lied to me," she said. "You said you'd never slept with her."

"I didn't say that. I just didn't say I had," he answered.

"That's lying," she said.

"No, that's just not telling all of it. There's a difference," he said.

"You're walking a fine line," she said.

"Maybe," he conceded. "But there's still a difference." He paused, letting a smile edge his lips. "If I'd told you, would you have backed off?" he asked.

"Of course," she said crisply.

"Now who's lying?" he asked evenly.

She glared back for a long moment and then her arms were around his neck, her lips pressing hard on his. "I am, damn you," she murmured. His hand cupped one long breast as she led him into the house. Some clouds do have a silver lining, in more ways than one, he reflected. This one certainly did.

LOOKING FORWARD!
**The following is the opening
section from the next novel in the exciting**
Trailsman **series from Signet:**

THE TRAILSMAN #204

THE LEAVENWORTH EXPRESS

*April 1859, Kansas Territory, where the gold fields
turned the hearts of some men black.*

As if it wasn't bad enough being left on foot, he was
on foot with a woman along. In town, in the saloon, in
bed, she was welcome, but out here, where the terrain
was flat and hard and he wanted to be able to move
fast, she was a hindrance. The only good thing about
having her along was that they were able to keep each
other warm at night.

Also, she carried some supplies, but not much. It
was left to Fargo to carry his rifle and saddlebags and
nothing else. Whatever meager supplies had been on
the stage were in a sack being carried by Karen, but
not without complaint. In fact, all she'd done all day
for the past three days was complain.

"Fargo," she said. "I can't go on."

"Yes, you can."

"I can't," she said. "I'm exhausted."

"We've got to keep moving, Karen."

"What makes you think you're going to catch up to them on foot?"

"I'm not," he said. "What I'm going to do on foot is get to a town where I can get a horse and then catch up to them."

"And then what?"

"And then get back what they stole, and bring them in to hang for killing Zack Wheeler."

Wheeler had been driving the stage when they got into trouble. It was the inaugural run for the fledgling stage line, the Leavenworth and Pike's Peak Express Company. They were going to run between Fort Leavenworth in the Kansas Territory to the Kansas gold fields. They had hired Fargo to ride along because part of their first run included the payroll for the mines. They wanted to make sure the first run was a success so that they could continue on from there.

It was Fargo's job to make sure the payroll got to the mines safely, and he still intended to see to it, even though the payroll had taken a short detour.

"Fargo," she whined, "we have to stop."

"No, we don't, Karen," he said. "Not until we reach there."

"Where?"

He pointed ahead of them where, on the horizon, he could make out the silhouette of a town. The sun was going down behind it, and it wasn't much more than shadows right now, but it was a town, he could see that.

"Thank God," Karen said. "Maybe they'll have baths, and a bed."

"And a horse," Fargo said, "and a telegraph line."

"Fargo," she said, "you don't intend to take me with you while you track those robbers down, do you?"

"No," he said. "I don't. You can stay here, or try to make your way back to Fort Leavenworth, or you can go on. It doesn't matter to me."

They walked along, drawing closer to the town, and now her silence was petulant rather than complaining.

"It's not my fault," she said finally.

"What isn't?"

"That I'm whiny and crabby. Any woman would be if she was forced to walk for three days."

"I'm sure you're right."

"You shouldn't hold it against me," she said. "You have to admit we had fun in town."

"Yes," he said, "we did, we had a lot of fun in town . . ."

Fargo turned over in bed and stared down at the girl lying next to him. She was on her back, and the bed-sheet was down around her waist. He admired the compact, tight body that he knew from personal experience contained boundless energy. She was young, in her early twenties, and her taut breasts had no sag to them, even though she was lying on her back. Her skin was pale, her nipples rosy in hue, erect even in sleep. Was she dreaming of him? If she was he was about to make her dreams come true . . . again.

Fargo had arrived in Fort Leavenworth four days earlier, and had met the girl—Karen—that evening. She worked in the saloon known only as #5, one of five girls who were serving drinks while the place was open, and making their own way when it closed. That night Fargo brought her back to his hotel room with him, and she had been coming back every night since. The only difference was, that first night he had paid her.

That first night she had surprised and delighted him with her energy and enthusiasm. In return—according to what she told him afterward—he had made her dreams come true.

"How did I do that?" he asked.

"I was dreaming that a man would come to town, a good-looking man who knew how to treat a woman, and that I wouldn't be stuck with some fat, smelly drifter or storekeeper."

"Well, then," he'd said, "I was happy to be of service, ma'am."

And he had been "of service" every night since.

Now, on their fourth morning together, she smiled in her sleep as he leaned over and kissed first one nipple, then the other. He drew them into his mouth, rolled them with his tongue, then sucked as much of them into his mouth as he could. She moaned and stretched, and he withdrew from her so he could watch. He'd learned over the past few mornings that she stretched quite a bit upon waking, and he enjoyed watching her lithe, taut body go through the motions of waking up.

"Good morning," she said, smiling up at him.

"Good morning," he said, and bent to his task again.

She moaned as his mouth roamed over her body,

waking her up. He tongued her deep navel, ran his nose through her pubic hair, then touched his tongue to her, tasting her. She caught her breath and wrapped her fingers in his hair, pressing his face to her. She moaned louder and began to grind her firm butt into the sheets as he devoured her.

Without allowing her to ride out the waves of pleasure that were wracking her body, he slid atop her and rammed his rigid penis into her. She was wet and hot, and he slid in easily.

"Oooh, my God," she groaned, "ooh, yes, Fargo, yes . . ."

Her orgasm, which she thought was over, seemed to go on and on, and he took her in long, hard strokes. He slid his hands beneath her so he could cup her buttocks and pull her to him each time he drove himself into her. She wrapped her arms and legs around him, raked his back with her nails, and sank her teeth into his shoulder. The bed began to move, but neither of them noticed it. They didn't care if anyone below them, or on either side of them, could hear them. She began to moan and cry out, and he started to grunt from the effort of fucking her.

"Jesus, yes," she said, urging him on, "oh yes, Fargo, harder . . . faster . . . don't stop . . . oooooohh . . ."

She began to buck beneath him as one orgasm ran into another, something she had never experienced with a man before, whether she was sleeping with them for business or pleasure.

"Oooh, God," she said, and then began to beat on his back with her fists, saying, "Stopstopstop!"

"Now you want me to stop?" he asked, puzzled.

"Yes!" she almost shouted. "I want to take you in my mouth."

"I think we can arrange that," he said. He withdrew his throbbing, engorged penis from her. It was slick with her juices and felt cold as the air hit it.

"On your back!" she commanded.

"Hurry," he said, "I'm cold."

"Not for long," she said.

She slithered down between his legs. Her tongue ran along his shaft. Then suddenly she opened wide and swooped down on him and the heat of her mouth closed around him.

"Yesss," he said as she began to suck him, her head bobbing up and down. She kept one hand wrapped around the base of him, while she fondled his testicles with the other, finding tender little spots with her fingertips. She rode him with her mouth, sucking him wetly, greedily until he felt the rush building up in his legs, flooding toward a release until finally he erupted inside her mouth. She peppered his thighs and crotch with light little butterfly kisses and was shocked to see that he was still hard.

"Not still," he told her, "again."

"You're an amazing man," she said, rubbing her fingers over him, then taking him in her fist and pumping him. She did this slowly at first, then faster and faster until she once again had him on the verge of an explosion. She released him then, raised herself above him, and sat on him, taking his length deep inside of her.

"Oh, ooh, you're so big, this is . . . glorious," she

said as she rode him up and down, her hands pressed down onto his belly for leverage as she rose and fell on him. The bed began to jump again as she did this, and it was only later, when they got out of bed, that they realized how much it had moved across the room.

Finally he was ready again, and he went off inside her. She felt as if there were thousands of tiny hot needles inside her. She closed her eyes, bit her lip, threw her head back, and enjoyed every second of it, milking him with her wet insides until he was drained dry again. She literally fell off him then, and laid down beside him, exhausted.

"God," she said, "oh, my God."

"Are you done?" he asked.

She slapped his side and said, "Don't tease me. Even you couldn't get ready again after that . . . could you?"

"You never know," he said, turning toward her, "until you try."

PENGUIN PUTNAM

—————————————————— online

Your Internet gateway to a virtual environment with hundreds of entertaining and enlightening books from Penguin Putnam Inc.

While you're there get the latest buzz on the best authors and books around—

Tom Clancy, Patricia Cornwell, W.E.B. Griffin, Nora Roberts, William Gibson, Robin Cook, Brian Jacques, Catherine Coulter, Stephen King, Jacquelyn Mitchard and many more!

Penguin Putnam Online is located at
http://www.penguinputnam.com

• •

PENGUIN PUTNAM
NEWS

Every month you'll get an inside look at our upcoming books and new features on our site. This is an ongoing effort on our part to provide you with the most interesting and up-to-date information about our books and authors.

Subscribe to Penguin Putnam News at
http://www.penguinputnam.com/ClubPPI